M000209526

LOVE, LOSS, & GHOSTS

Love, Loss, & Ghosts

STORIES

CAROL WESTREICH SOLOMON

LUMINARE PRESS
WWW.LUMINAREPRESS.COM

Love, Loss, & Ghosts: Stories
Copyright © 2020 by Carol Westreich Solomon

All rights reserved. This book or any portion thereof may not be reproduced or used in any manner whatsoever without the express written permission of the publisher, except for the use of brief quotations in a book review.

Carol Solomon is supported in part by funding from the Montgomery County Government and the Arts & Humanities Council of Montgomery County.

Printed in the United States of America

Cover Design by Melissa K. Thomas

Luminare Press
442 Charnelton St.
Eugene, OR 97401
www.luminarepress.com

LCCN: 2020919553
ISBN: 978-1-64388-494-3

To Morris

Contents

The following stories have previously appeared in other publications:

"Playoffs" (*Loch Raven Review,* 2019)

"The Fixer" (*Bethesda Magazine,* 2019)

"Thieves" *(Pen-in-Hand, 2019)*

"Mother's Day" (*Little Patuxent Review,* 2017)

"Heartache" *(Persimmon Tree,* 2014)

"Reunion" (*Poetica,* 2014)

"Wading in the Water" (*Pen-in-Hand,* 2017)

Lost

I am only a mile from my condo in the planned community where I have lived for forty-five years. On my morning walk, I cross the treeless field as the sun bears down and my sweat stinks like a child after playing outdoors. In March, this walk invigorated me. Now, in the heat of July, it depletes. Blue plastic gloves dot the landscape, synthetic flowers signaling an unnatural world where life exists in digital flickers on a screen, and blue gloves and face masks protect us from the enemy—each other. Somewhere along the wooded path behind the Elsyian Meadows townhouses, I lose myself.

The date? Who knows? The time? Time folds and bends back on itself. It could be yesterday, tomorrow, dawn, dusk. I know I'm walking because keys in my pocket thump against my hip as one foot labors to replace another. I know I'm breathing because steam coats my glasses. But where am I going? Tall pine trees block the sun and hide anything that could orient me. The needle-matted path offers no clue.

A dog barks. Someone calls out, "Come on, Charlie." I turn, hoping to see a face, any face. But that someone—a woman with a floppy straw hat—has turned away as a dog pulls her in a different direction. Even if she were still here, she would be faceless. I can't recall what lies behind a mask. Are lips opened or closed while someone walks, the ends curved up or flat? Does a nose twitch or remain passive when someone speaks? Can you tell someone's age by the condition of her cheeks—plump or sunken, pinkish or gray, smooth or mottled?

The trees grow taller, turning black, leaning toward each other, taunting with their ability to touch, trapping me, whoever I am, whoever I was. But habit pulls me forward down the curving, twisting path beneath the dark ceiling. I go left, then right, then double back, the trees wobble, my head spins. Like Hansel and Gretel following their bread crumbs, I try to follow the blue flowers back to where I started, back to myself, but there are too many gloves scattered about. Stuck in undulating darkness, I cling to a moving tree, slide to the ground, and rest against its trunk, tucking my head downward until the spinning stops and the trees stay still. Above, birds twitter, bleat, honk. Below, at the tree base, darkness tempers the heat and the humidity, and a faint breeze cools my sweaty face.

Alone, lost, I look up for resurrection and from behind the tree tops, watch the sky emerge like an empty Zoom screen. Light flickers. I enter Gallery View. My father—dead for decades—appears, his hair slicked back, his mouth moving, the words slightly delayed, his golden voice tinny. My daughter sitting poolside in San Diego, granddaughter on her lap, waves. "Say hi," she instructs. I reach up to hold Ella's tiny hand and grasp air. My son, long hair pulled in ponytail, gives a thumbs up in front of a green screen of Paris. My husband, buried when mourners could share a common shovel, looks untouched by death as he blows a kiss. I long for little arms to fling around my knees, fingers to caress my sagging breasts, hands to lovingly cup my face. I'd even settle for a perfunctory hug after a party, an arm around my shoulders at synagogue, the casual handshake of a new acquaintance, the accidental brush of a stranger's arm in a theatre seat.

I remember who I was, who I am, what is lost, what I must find. One by one, we leave the meeting. The flickering screen disappears. The trees still block the sun. The path still curves unexpectedly. The blue plastic gloves still dot the landscape. I cannot touch the people I love, cannot even be with those still alive, cannot go to a party or the synagogue or the theatre. But I can make them live and restore my life. I can write.

Reunion

E thel had exactly one hour and thirty-five minutes to finish the sixty-fifth birthday collage for her husband before he returned from the gym with the man she paid to be his friend.

"Thank goodness for the workouts," she thought. If not for the twice weekly workouts, she would never have been able to do all the things needed for his surprise party, what with Steve following her from room to room at home as if he might lose her. With her well-manicured fingers, Ethel smoothed the gold and burgundy ribbon around the perimeter of the poster, making sure no bubbles or bulges or slivers of white foam board marred the effect. She was sure Steve would recognize the colors of the Washington football team. Color still affected him deeply, like the russet and yellow leaves outside their townhouse.

"I love that gold time of the year," he had announced when the paid friend had arrived in sweatpants.

I love it, too, Ethel had thought as she had watched Steve bounce down the sidewalk to the waiting car, kicking the leaves like a kid. Something about the golden season lifted her mood—the season of Sukkot, which celebrated the harvest before the winter. This birthday was Steve's Sukkot—the celebration of his life, all sixty-five years of it, much more bounty than he had expected. His father, after all, had died way too young at fifty, and Steve had lived his life as if he too would die a pre-Medicare death.

Only two spots for photos remained on the board. One spot next to their formal wedding picture with Steve's eyes glazed from a 103-degree fever that limited his participation to picture-taking and the ceremony and left her a solitary celebrant. And the other spot next to their snapshot in the parking lot of Two Cousins Pizza, where Steve placed his hand tenderly on her puffy middle, the beginnings of their first child. They'd been so pumped with joy, anyone could read it in her sassy smile and his impish grin. After six months of trying, which had seemed an eternity, finally there was to be a baby. Jakey. Jacob Bradley Ackerman. Yacov Baruch—named after Steve's father and her grandfather.

She wondered if she should put a picture of Jakey on the board. Would its presence make Steven sad and remind guests of Jakey's absence from the party? Or would its absence create more pain as if Jakey had never existed? One hour and fifteen minutes left. Make a choice, Ethel, she told herself. She picked a picture of Alisha's Bat Mitzvah with the four of them so gussied up that they were barely recognizable, then slathered the back with Elmer's Glue and pressed the photo firmly to the foam board before she could change her mind.

She tried not to think of Jakey as she massaged the glue bubbles under his curly black hair. But what harm was there in remembering eyes that sparkled like black diamonds and a laugh that could turn a seder from stiff to celebratory?

A car door slammed, followed by different laughter—a high-pitched laugh accompanied by a playful shriek. It was Alisha and little Sophie. She'd forgotten they were coming by to plan while Steve was at the gym. As the key turned in the front door, Ethel grabbed the picture of Steve tossing a football to Jakey, her favorite of the two of them. The floating ball's unbroken arc connected their outstretched hands. She tucked the picture furtively beneath the foam board as if concealing it could bury her thoughts. But it was too late.

"You're crying," announced Alisha as she entered the dining room. "It's that damn Jake again."

THE METRO TRAIN HURTLED FROM THE SHADY GROVE station toward Washington, packed with commuters and their bulging backpacks and briefcases. Most closed their eyes, reclaiming a lost half hour of sleep, oblivious to the frequent jerks and squeals that suggested an impending derailment.

She stared out the window at the unfamiliar landscape, the dirty junkyards and hidden trash bins of the suburb she thought she knew so well. She hugged her brown and black purse packed with flyers with Jakey's face and her contact information. Despite Alisha's vehement, know-it-all insistence that Ethel was "looking for trouble," Ethel knew what she had been denying for weeks. There could be no true celebration of Steve's birthday without their son. Even though it had been two years since his disappearance without a single sighting or call, she would find him and bring him to his father's party while a reunion was still possible. She would do on her own, what they had paid the detective $5,000 to attempt two years ago—visit all the sites in the city where a man without money or work might be sleeping.

Where to begin? Ethel couldn't imagine Jakey living under an elevated train track and warming his hands over fires in discarded metal bins. If he was living on the streets of DC, surely he would have claimed a friendly heating grate somewhere near the Smithsonian, where on a bitter day he could tuck his possessions behind a well-pruned bush and visit Mary Cassatt's mother and child pictures at the National Gallery.

The train lurched to its Rockville stop, and more sleep-deprived commuters wedged into the car. She wondered if Steve had awakened yet and found Alisha and Sophie, his "sitters," watching Sesame Street in the family room. She imagined Sophie climbing on his lap and sprinkling kisses all over his unshaved face. Would he believe Alisha when she said mom had a doctor's appointment in the city and would be gone most of the day? Or would he wander around the house, like a lost child, knocking on every bathroom door in search of Ethel?

By the time the train jerked its way to a tentative stop at Adams Morgan, the people boarding the train were no longer tired mothers and fathers headed to their government jobs. Instead, the newest boarders were skinny, bare-legged girls in ballet flats with silky hair cascading over form-fitting jackets. Or tousle-haired young men with meticulous stubble, clutching a Starbucks coffee, as they headed to their jobs at non-profits. Jakey would be getting on the train here if he had finished his degree at Georgetown in International Economics. He would be living with one of the bare-legged girls, who would be pressing him about commitment while he explored possibilities to make a difference in Africa.

At the Smithsonian stop, Ethel left the Metro and stepped on the escalator to the Mall. When the tunnel-effect winds pushed her back, she grabbed the railing for balance, then clutched her purse close to her body so that other riders wouldn't dislodge it. At the top, Ethel surveyed the Mall. It had been years since she and Steve had last visited the museums, back when he could still drive and they would park at a stone-covered lot now replaced by another huge government building. The Mall was larger than she recalled, two rows of massive museums flanking the vast expanse of grass that stretched from the Capitol to the Washington Monument, enough grassy space to accommodate hundreds of thousands of people at a protest or a folklife festival. And around each museum—trees, shrubs, benches, heating grates—too many to count—where a person disconnected from the real world could temporarily anchor himself. Still, she could not, would not, be deterred by the size of her challenge.

She walked briskly toward the American History Museum, the closest of the buildings, picking up her pace as the wind whipped her salt and pepper hair. She reached up to smooth the hair in place, but another gust scrambled it as soon as she removed her hand. What a mess she must be. Not how she wanted to look when she found Jakey. Opposite the museum entrance, a bearded man with dirt-crusted dreadlocks stretched out on a bench, enfolded in a camouflage sleeping bag. When he finally stirred, Ethel unzipped her purse and removed a picture of Jakey taken when he entered Georgetown, the last good picture she had of him.

"Excuse me."

The man grunted and shifted position.

"Excuse me. May I ask you a question?"

"Huh?" He turned toward her, propped himself on his elbow, and stared at her with terrifying glassy eyes. Eyes like those of the residents of Jakey's group home as they sat on sagging sofas watching game shows, as if movement might unleash their demons.

"Have you seen him?" She stretched out her arm and thrust the flier at the man whose wild odor made her want to gag. He squinted, then looked up at her face.

"It's Jesus," he announced and plopped back down. "Not interested in finding him." He closed his eyes and mumbled something that sounded like profanity.

No surprise that he didn't know Jakey. He wasn't at all the type of man Jakey would associate with.

Around the corner a stocky thirtyish woman bundled in a khaki jacket sang at the top of her lungs a vaguely familiar song that Ethel had heard in Alisha's car.

"Just because I'm losing
Doesn't mean I'm lost
Doesn't mean I'll stop
Doesn't mean I'm in a cross.
Just because I'm hurting
Doesn't mean I'm hurt
Doesn't mean I didn't get what I deserve
No better and no worse."

At the crescendo, the woman waved her hands to the sky, then waited for the applause of her one-person audience.

"Lovely voice," said Ethel with a smile signaling that she was no threat. The woman bowed and took a deep breath. But before she could launch another off-key song, Ethel held out a flier. "My son. He's lost, like in the song. Have you seen him around?"

"I could use a few bucks for a hot dog and a cuppa coffee."

Ethel rummaged in her purse and extracted a five dollar bill.

The woman grabbed the money and shoved it down her bra. "Can't take chances. Never know who else saw the money."

"Have you seen my boy?" Ethel straightened the wrinkled flier so the woman could get a better look.

"Might of. Don't know for sure. Hunger makes my eyes fuzz up." The woman raised the palm of her hand.

It felt like extortion to Ethel, but what was another five if she got an answer? The woman shoved the additional money down her bra, then read every inch of the flier like a newspaper. "Nope. Not my type." Ethel knew she'd been taken.

She hadn't expected the search to be easy, but the diversity of street dwellers stirred a dizzying mixture of fear and nurturing. The young white woman with weeds woven through her greasy hair, who could become quite lovely with a bath and a shampoo, almost like the bare-legged girls on the subway. The old black man missing half a leg and half his teeth, who petted a snarling mutt on his lap. The hollow-eyed man with a pair of broken glasses, who called out to her, "My biological mother" and stroked her face. When she recoiled, he whispered so she could barely hear him, "Kick me." She took only one break, about two-ish, to enter the museum so she could rest her cranky knee and get coffee and a sandwich. But when she stared at the plastic-encased tuna sandwich, she couldn't eat it. Instead, she stuffed it in her pocket in case she found Jakey. And when she didn't find Jakey, not even someone who had seen Jakey, she found the hollowed-eyed man with the broken glasses and said, "Here's a sandwich from your biological mother."

When the government workers started streaming toward the Metro and the sky faded to gray, Ethel waded back through the waves of people toward the bearded man on the bench. Maybe after all, he had recognized her son. Maybe Jakey had grown long hair and turned to religious rants like a Jesus of the street dwellers. But when she returned to the bench, even the bearded man had gone somewhere for the evening.

IN THEIR HALF-EMPTY KING-SIZE BED, STEVE WAS SNORing. But Ethel couldn't dislodge the rock in her heart. There would be no Jakey at the party. Probably no Jakey while Steve could still recognize him. Maybe no Jakey ever.

She crept from her bed and tiptoed down the carpeted stairs to the kitchen for some tea. The cold heaviness of her soul felt like the night the group home called with the news that Jake had slipped out, and they were so, so sorry to tell her that he had failed to return. At first she'd thought he'd make his way back to their townhouse. But when he didn't, part of her was relieved. She remembered before the group home. The wild mood swings, the crazy accusations, the meds flushed down the toilet, the shouts from his room at all hours of the night, the occasional physical altercations. She remembered, too, how long it had taken for Steve to agree that Jake needed a good group home—for all of their sake. But when the first group home didn't work out and the second home folded, they had been lucky to find any place at all to take him in.

"Get me out of here," Jake had begged when they visited. "I'm dying."

In her yellow kitchen, on the countertop she had updated with granite as an anniversary gift to herself, the knives with their rich wooden handles looked so inviting.

The largest knife she kept especially sharp to slice brisket on the holidays. It would pierce so easily into her chest and allow the rock to escape. She slid the knife from its holder and tested its cold, sharp edge.

No, she decided. Not now. She slid the knife back into its holder, poured water into the teapot, turned on the stove, and waited for the water to boil.

THE DINING ROOM TABLE, ANCHORED AT EACH END BY a ginger-colored potted chrysanthemum, groaned under the weight of the sliced turkey and hot brisket in silver chafing dishes, the quinoa salad for those who were health conscious and the potato salad for those who weren't, the marinated asparagus, the Waldorf salad, the tiny whole-wheat rolls for those who absolutely must have some bread. Ethel, who had long subscribed to her mother's belief that ample food equaled love, had also filled every space on the dessert table with French macaroons, black and white cookies, marble cake, assorted pastries from the nearby Chocolate Palace, and the pièce de résistance—a white chocolate mousse sheet cake with the words *Happy 65th, Steve.* No one would leave hungry.

When she passed by the birthday collage in the foyer, she turned on her high wattage smile to pulverize the rock that was threatening to re-form. She had removed the pictures of Jakey from the birthday collage, using her brisket knife to scrape away any tell-tale glue residue. A sixth-grade photo of Steve with a strange cowlick and a recent photo of Steve holding Sophie on his lap took their place. Still, she knew what wasn't there.

"What a spread," announced her brother-in-law with his overflowing plate.

"Love, love, love what you've done to the kitchen," said a cousin who hadn't bothered to call since Passover.

No one said the J-word. But she imagined there had been long discussions in their cars on the drive over about whether it was best to ask about the missing son or pretend he never crossed their minds. And someone in each car must have concluded by saying, "Thank G-d, it isn't our kid. I don't know how they stand it." Once or twice she detected a look of pity from someone studying the collage. And she noticed eye signals from husband to wife as they finished what passed for a conversation with Steve.

Time for a glass of wine to dissolve the rock. Flash that smile, Ethel. The laughter, the incessant banter, her son-in-law sitting in the corner of the kitchen to tweet strangers about meaningless football games, the racing children who threatened to topple her tables, the cumulative effect of four glasses of wine—together they were making Ethel unbelievably exhausted. Her legs felt heavy, her mind empty, her mouth sluggish. Soon everyone would be gone. All but Steve and herself. And soon he would be gone, too.

She grabbed a half empty tray of French pastries and excused herself to go down to the basement refrigerator to replenish the platter. Downstairs, where the sounds of the furnace muffled the manufactured gaiety of the party, she allowed her smile to disappear and permitted herself two minutes to remember Jakey. This time she remembered him at five in his navy striped polo shirt as he leaned against their slender dogwood tree that she had decorated with crepe paper and balloons in honor of his first day of kindergarten. Before he even stepped inside the school, he was reading and full of questions about spaceships and American presidents and tornadoes. Every year she had decorated that tree at the start of school for Jakey, until in middle school he felt embarrassed by such things and Ethel had stopped, though Alisha had begged for just one more year.

"Kick me," she said to the imaginary Jakey. "You don't know what's going to happen later, but you're going to hate me. So just go ahead and kick me now."

When her two minutes had passed, she flipped on her smile and started to carry the replenished platter up the steps. Five steps from the top she heard people all talking at once—very excited—and a loud voice, Steve's voice, calling out, "He's here. Jakey's here." The platter clattered to the ground, mini éclairs and cream puffs and pecan tarts tumbling down the steps. Ethel's legs folded under her, and she collapsed on the step, squashing a stray éclair.

The flier. Someone had shown Jakey the flier. Or maybe the wind, guided by the spirit of G-d, had blown a discarded flier to the very grate where Jakey set up his bedroll for the night. A joy that she had forgotten propelled her up the stairs into the hallway. See, she told Alisha mentally, I told you it would only happen if I tried.

A crowd had gathered around Steve, who was gleefully repeating, "My boy. My Jakey!"

"Let me through," begged Ethel as she pushed aside the people blocking her vision.

Alisha, her face twisted in anger and sadness, was holding Sophie, who had started to cry. "Stop it, Dad. You're scaring her."

"Where's Jake?" asked Ethel. "Where's my son?"

The guests avoided Ethel's eyes. Where was her boy? Had they frightened him, too? Had he escaped out the front door? As the crowd parted, Ethel saw Steve pointing enthusiastically at the collage. He was smiling at the picture of the two of them in the parking lot at Two Cousins Pizza. Then, before Alisha could stop him, he leaned over until his lips touched the picture and kissed Ethel's puffy belly.

"My boy."

Ethel felt a flutter in her stomach, like the gentle kick of a baby. She heard a rich, melodious laugh with the deepening tones of a teenager fill the room. She saw a young man with dark curly hair and eyes like diamonds standing just inside the doorway, his right arm stretched high above him.

"Throw it to me, Dad," he called out.

And the love in Steve's kiss hurtled through time, piercing physical reality, reaching a higher reality where their son, their Jakey, would always live.

Mother's Day

Kimmy sat frozen on the floor of her bedroom closet, breathing rapidly like when she'd reached the final stretch of her cross country run in high school. Kailey and Krista yelped and wailed in the background. Kailey was likely climbing on the sofa trying to reach all the track trophies and wedding pictures on the shelf next to it. Krista was probably lying on her playmat and bellowing while her arms and legs flailed. Kimmy listened for a crash. But all she heard through the closed door was the cries of her two girls.

She wished it was six o'clock. Then maybe Earl would walk in the door and scoop up the girls, one in each arm, and she could escape from her closet and Earl could throw her a half-smile meant only for her. But it was three, and Earl was working late again tonight. When he did come home, he'd be sweaty and too tired to do anything but gulp down a beer and whatever she put on his plate. By then she would've bathed the girls and put on their jammies and sung them their special songs and given Krista her last bottle until her screaming started again at two a.m.

Only one voice—Krista's—still pierced the closet door. Maybe Kailey had stole Krista's blankey and was waving it around the room. Or maybe, oh please no, no, no, maybe Kailey was poking her finger in Krista's eye or smashing the baby on the head with her doll. She should get out there—check what was going on—save Krista. But the stuffiness and darkness of the closet comforted her. Besides, she needed to catch her breath first. She couldn't walk without breathing.

The babies had come one after the other, eleven months apart, the first one planned and prayed for, the second an accident when Earl pulled Kimmy into bed as soon as the ob-gyn gave her the okay and little Kailey finally, mercifully fell asleep. He'd forgotten to buy condoms; she hadn't yet filled the prescription for her birth control pills, too tired to even think about sex. But Earl had been drooling for weeks as she nursed the baby, so she just welcomed him back where he was longing to be.

Kimmy's hand accidentally brushed against her wedding gown encased in a protective bag as if somehow she'd be needing it again. She remembered the dress' mermaid shape that made her look like a star in *People* magazine and her once-upon-a-time taut body that made her honeymoon negligee slide right off. She remembered the makeout sessions in Earl's pickup truck when their breath smoked up the windshield and his musky sweat mixed with hers. She remembered powerful legs and lungs propelling her over country roads to the golden trophy waiting at the end. Ages ago. Before the lingering stink of dirty diapers clung to her.

The sudden silence outside the door terrified her, gave her the shakes. It was worse than the crying, which at least meant that the girls were both alive, even if they were bleeding or had broken their arms or swallowed her medicine. The silence said what the world would say. She should have been a better mother. If she had been a better mother, her girls would be alive.

Her eyelids drooped, her breathing deepened. The meds must be kicking in.

THE CHIME OF HER CELL PHONE WOKE HER. HOW LONG had she been asleep in the closet? The light spilling beneath the closet door told her it was still afternoon. What was she doing wearing Earl's blue flannel shirt over her t-shirt that reeked of baby spitup? Where were the girls? Where was the phone?

Then Kimmy remembered it was on the other side of the closet door tucked in the diaper bag, which she'd taken with her hours ago to Walmart for more formula. She listened to the cell chime and chime and then click off. More silence. Then it chimed again and again.

Probably Earl calling during a break to check what she was making for dinner. There wasn't going to be any dinner. Then she remembered—or any daughters.

"Kimmy," he'd said back when he slipped the sparkling, almost-diamond on her finger, "it'll be the best. You and me and later a real family." Something that he'd lost when his father walked away and stayed away for more than twenty years, creating cracks in Earl she was still trying to fill.

"Oh, baby, we'll have a house full of kids," Kimmy had said as she lassoed Earl with her bejeweled hand, kissed him hard on the lips, and then smothered his whole face with her famous kisslets.

"I love your kisslets," Earl had whispered as he stroked her long hair. "You wanna know why? Because each one says you love me and the love just keeps bubbling up because there's so much of it."

"Surprise, Earl. It ain't bubbling anymore," Kimmy told her shirt as she yanked it off. She shoved Earl's shirt beneath his hunting boots. That would make him good and mad to have dirt clods all over his favorite shirt. She wished she had a scissors so she could cut the damn shirt to shreds.

Kimmy stared at the soft blue flannel, cowering beneath the boots. She had bought Earl the shirt for his birthday. When she rested her head on it as they watched t.v. on the rare occasions both girls were sleeping, she felt protected, secure. She was punishing the shirt for something that wasn't its fault. She pulled out the shirt and shook off the dirt. She held it up as if Earl had suddenly slipped into it.

"Oh, Earl, baby, it isn't your fault either. All you did was love me."

She saw the girls, silent and motionless, side by side in the living room as Earl would see them when he got home. Their round faces and downy curls covered by blood, that's how he'd always remember them. And he'd always remember her as the careless, cruel mother who let this happen. What would he say when he called the police? That his wife had let their kids kill each other. That his wife was hiding in the bedroom closet and wouldn't come out. That he didn't even want to open the door to let her out. That the sight of her would make him puke.

KIMMY DOZED OFF AGAIN. HER SLEEP-DEPRIVED NIGHTS and the stuffiness of the closet—barely wide enough to qualify as a walk-in—took their toll. This time the deepness of Kimmy's sleep carried her away from the horror of her silent daughters. Instead, she saw her young self with a ponytail and Cinderella barrettes surrounded by a procession of dolls. Chubby cloth dolls with mechanical baby cries. Water-sucking and water-producing dolls with oversized plastic heads. Skinny, top-heavy Barbies balancing on perpendicular shoes. Miniature dolls cupped in giant hands controlling their movement.

"Ma-ma, Ma-ma," one big-headed doll cried, lifting her plastic arms toward young Kimmy.

"Oh, Ken, kiss me," Barbie begged to an invisible Ken doll as she swished her synthetic hair.

As young Kimmy played the part of each doll, her voice changed pitch and tone—whining, demanding, seductive, obstinate. Suddenly young Kimmy was sprouting octopus tentacles as she reached out simultaneously to rapidly multiplying dolls until her young self bobbed and sank, swallowed up by the grotesque doll parade.

"Mama! Mama!" This time Kimmy heard her own voice, that of a woman lost in her own closet, who could barely breathe. She saw the face of her own mother, beautiful, distracted. How she longed for someone to lift her up, cradle her, kiss her.

"Mama! Mama!" Now not Kimmy's voice, but a high-pitched toddler's voice—halting, muffled, far away.

"Mama! Mama!" Little hands pounded on a door.

The innocent desperation of the voice pulled Kimmy out of the dream. Sweet Jesus, at least one of the girls was alive. Kimmy knew she needed to stand, to open the closet door and then the bedroom door. But her rubbery legs wouldn't let her.

"Coming, Kailey," she called out.

"Mama." Her world in one word.

Kimmy strained to lift herself, grabbing for support the

hem of the dress she'd worn to Kailey's christening, but she slid back to the floor, a helpless blob amidst shoes and dirty clothes overflowing the laundry basket.

"Mama's coming, Kailey," she called again.

Kimmy propped herself up and alternating cheek-to-cheek scooched her butt across the closet floor. Past Earl's hunting boots. Past their dirty underwear that she meant to wash today. Past the fading t-shirt that said Bardwell Cross Country. She had to get out, save Kailey, feed her, hold her, find Krista and see if she was still breathing, call the hospital if she was hurt.

Finally, she touched the door and grabbed the wood frame to inch herself off the ground. Once again, she slid backward and fell to the floor powerless. Two closed doors separated her from her surviving daughter and the silent baby. Two closed doors that she wanted to open but couldn't.

She heard her cross country coach telling her to dig deep, to find whatever was at her core that would take her past the wall that she inevitably hit running up the hill near Bardwell High. Dig deep, beyond the tedium. Dig deep, beyond the exhaustion. Dig deep, beyond the part-time husband. Dig deep, to her buried self. Dig deep, to Earl with his dimpled chin planting himself in her heart and twisting his roots around every vein and artery. Dig deep, to the doctor placing Kailey in her arms and Earl kissing her head, making the circle complete. Dig deep, to soft skin and sweet milk breath.

The rubbery legs became the muscled legs of the cross country runner, allowing Kimmy to stand and open the door.

Heartache

Becky listened to the oxygen forcing its way along narrow tubing into her nose and then down to her lungs, filling her with enough air to tell her husband Barry what he had a right to know about that night twenty years ago, when she and Rabbi Finkelstein had met to wrestle with a leadership crisis in their religious school. Barry had handed the phone to her quickly, then excused himself to get coffee. Usually he welcomed callers as a diversion from their hospital existence. But this time he had disappeared for half an hour, leaving Becky alone to converse with the intruder from the past.

Now Becky reached for her husband's hand through the metal bed railing, felt only air, then noticed his hands were tucked in his pants pockets. It was the first time he hadn't physically been there for her since she had awakened one week ago with unstoppable coughing. Even as he called 911, his free hand had clutched hers, assuring her that help was on the way. In the ER as she had struggled to catch her breath and fought the nurse's effort to position an oxygen mask, Barry had calmed her, "Becky, let them do it. It'll help, Babe." And when the doctors told them yesterday that she had a tumor devouring her heart that would in two or three weeks cut off her ability to breathe, and that sadly, there was no treatment when the tumor was this big, at least no

Carol Solomon

treatment that would appreciably extend her life—even then Barry had made her feel in his enveloping embrace that nothing truly bad would ever happen because he was here.

Just as she started to whisper "I love you" so as to erase the voice of Rabbi Finkelstein, her children and their spouses descended upon the room with an overstuffed bouquet of hydrangeas and artificial laughter. Then ensued the discussion of where to put the puffy flowers—on the nightstand filled with a box of tissues and a vomit bucket—or under the hanging hazardous waste box on a counter already cluttered with wilting daisies from her book club and a stiff arrangement of roses from the Sisterhood of Congregation Beth Israel and drooping daffodils from someone (she couldn't recall who). No more flowers, she wanted to scream.

Allison, the oldest, was directing the placement of the flowers and the medical accessories, as if to achieve the feng shui most amenable to miraculous, spontaneous recovery, her voice reverberating like a Sousa march. Jayme, the middle child, focused her brown eyes on Becky as if death would snatch Becky away immediately if she didn't monitor her mother's every breath. Like a Yiddish lullaby, Jayme's voice said, "Mom, you don't need to worry. I'm worrying enough for us both." Andrew, the youngest, who was in the midst of an exhausting divorce, sank into Becky's wheelchair. From him there was no sound, only a silence that told Becky how much he needed her and how afraid he was to express that need, as if it might accelerate her death.

"Guess who just called?" she heard Barry ask amidst the tumult.

"Don't know," Jayme answered, "because just about everyone in existence has already called—even people I didn't know were still alive."

"That's a dumb thing to say, considering the circumstances," opined the older daughter, who always had something to say about everything.

"Rabbi Finkelstein. That's who called," asserted Becky between coughs, trying to head off a sibling confrontation.

"Rabbi Finkelstein?" asked Jayme. "Wow, that's a name I haven't heard for ages. How many years has he been gone from Beth Israel? Fifteen?"

"Twenty," corrected Andrew, who suddenly sat forward in the wheelchair. "I remember because it was my Bar Mitzvah and he left so unexpectedly that we had to hire a temporary rabbi who didn't even know me."

"Well, it was no loss, if you ask me," announced Allison.

"Enough," said Becky, wondering why Barry had even mentioned the phone call. Was he signaling that he knew the import of that call? "Enough about Rabbi Finkelstein. He heard I was sick," Becky managed, pausing to catch her breath. "He did a mitzvah. Forget the man's shortcomings." She turned toward Barry, but he averted his eyes.

After her daughters and their spouses and Andrew, and eventually even Barry had left her room, after the nurse's aide had removed the hospital dinner tray with its congealed, tasteless food, after the bustle of the evening blood pressure checks had subsided, Becky lay alone and contemplated the shortness of her days. Two or three weeks they had said yesterday. Which was it? And how did they know? On the MRI did her heart have a digital timer? The doctors' guess could no more measure her remaining days than measure the fullness of the years preceding the diagnosis.

At sixteen Becky had imagined a life of traveling and creating soaring music in concert halls and making love with iconoclastic men of various ethnicities. But choice by choice, she had constructed a life, which while not identical to her mother's unexceptional domesticity, resembled it in ways that would have pleased her mother, who had endured Becky's condescending comments. Still, Becky regretted few choices—certainly not the choice of Barry, a dependable man, who anchored her life in Northwest Baltimore and the Jewish domesticity she had disparaged. Her exotic travel had consisted of cruises to nondescript islands. Her creation of soaring music had morphed into teaching music in the religious school. Her love-making with assorted iconoclasts had been reduced to love-making with one man, her husband. With the exception, of course, of Rabbi Ezra Finklestein.

And what was she to do with the two or three weeks, or maybe—G-d willing—even more that she had left on this earth? What did she owe her children, her husband, herself—before her family shoveled dirt to fill the hole?

A medical monitor next door bleated. No feet scrambled down the hall to answer its urgent call. Were the nurses understaffed or just desensitized to the implications of the bleat? Or was the shofar-like sound calling her? The loud bleat had ceased, the problem attended to, no extra bustle signifying a code red. But sleep evaded Becky. In the shadows of her funereal room, she thought she saw the face of Rabbi Finkelstein. Not the lined face of a man in his sixties, but Ezra as she had seen him that night—his eyes ablaze, an almost Asian look to his brows which created an exotic lure.

"Rebecca," he whispered.

She closed her eyes. She would not be seduced a second time. But Ezra's face lingered.

Again, he whispered, "Rebecca," this time more urgently. "Rebecca, my special friend." It was the same words he had used that night. How many other women had he used that phrase with? But she could never ask, not even after their wisp of an affair had ended, because to ask would be to admit. That night, she had seen herself as the only one among his congregants who could understand his burdens and provide him peace.

For months, she had blamed her infidelity on Ezra. If he had not brushed his hand across her knee, she would have dreamed of him but never acted on that dream. But she, too, had brushed her hand subtly against his knee as she leaned over to pick up the papers she had dropped. She remembered, too, reddening when he told her how lonely he was, how his wife had little sympathy for his struggles when he returned home late after yet another rancorous board meeting. And then she had said, "Rabbi Finkelstein, you deserve better." As she had said it, she had thought of her bland life, her fractious children, the lost elasticity of her skin, and Barry, who had become as familiar as an old sweater.

She was not surprised when Ezra leaned in to kiss her forehead, like a benevolent father. She didn't push him away. When he tilted her chin in his hand, she could have stood and offered any one of a dozen excuses for a quick departure without making a scene. Instead, she had parted her lips. Rabbi Ezra Finkelstein had sins to atone for. But he had not forced Becky to lie with him on his pastoral sofa beneath the shelves of Torah commentaries. Even now, in this horrible room, she felt again the thrill of his taut, unfamiliar body.

When they had both come and she remembered again who she was, she had covered her body with her winter jacket, collected her clothes, and dashed into the ladies room to scrub her body with the pump soap and paper towels set out for congregants. She had not said goodbye, had not wanted to see Rabbi Finkelstein pulling up his pants. Grateful that Barry was out of town on business, she had showered three times at home, shampooing her hair each time, and had thrown every article of clothing into the washing machine at the hottest temperature—even her new woolen slacks.

When Rabbi Finkelstein called the next day regarding a meeting on what he said was "a critical matter," she had feigned illness. And when he called two days later to meet about the musical program for Purim, she had said that they could just talk on the phone. But for years, long after Rabbi Finkelstein had hastily tendered his resignation due to family concerns and moved with them to the other side of the country, she had remembered the scent of his skin and the tenaciousness of his lips.

MUCH TO EVERYONE'S SURPRISE THE DOCTORS announced in the morning that Becky would be discharged the following day, after arrangements could be made for a hospital bed and hospice care at home. The doctors had no more tricks in their repertoire. When Barry wheeled Becky up the hastily erected ramp to the porch of the home they had shared for forty years, the October air invigorated her. The blazing red leaves dressed up her aging home, concealing the drain spout in need of paint.

"Home," she said to Barry as he rubbed her neck.

"Home," he replied.

Allison sprang into action, rearranging the living room furniture to position the hospital bed to give Becky privacy, while including her in the family bustle. Barry guided Becky from the wheelchair to the bed, gently repositioned the oxygen in her nose, and fluffed the pillows so she was propped upright like a queen. Meanwhile Jayme dashed to the kitchen to reheat frozen chicken soup, leftover from the family's Rosh Hashannah feast. Only Andrew was missing, off at some important meeting with the lawyer to untangle the finances of his disintegrating marriage.

Surrounded by her framed wedding ketubah and pictures from the weddings and Bar and Bat Mitzvahs of her children, Becky felt like a fraudulent woman of valor. She recalled her own mother's death, when the whole family had encircled her mother's hospital bed while the women in her mother's prayer group had chanted Hebrew psalms. Slowly her mother's breathing had subsided until she was gone. The holiness of the moment of her passing and all the days leading up to it testified to the goodness of her mother's life. Becky's own life did not deserve a holy end.

"Mom, I bought a juicer and a cancer cookbook. I'm going to juice up some broccoli and asparagus and kale for you," Allison called from the kitchen, pulling Becky back to the here and now.

"Mmm," added Jayme. "How delicious. Raw vegetable juice and chicken soup."

Becky heard the hum of the juicer, probably Allison's response to her sister's sarcasm. "My friend's mother is still alive on this diet, two years after the doctors gave her six months at most," Allison shouted over the juicer.

"What's this all about?" Becky whispered to Barry, slightly nauseated at the thought of raw vegetable juice for lunch. "I'd rather have Thrashers fries." She could smell the sizzling oil of the classic Ocean City fries mixing with the fragrance of suntan lotion and the briny ocean breeze.

"She's holding on to you, Beck. She wants you here for her kids." Then Barry laughed, the first laugh she had heard from him in a week. "I could go for some fries, too. Maybe after Allison goes home to pick up the kids, I can sneak out to the mall and bring some back."

Becky nodded.

"And I'll take the blame if her nose detects them." He kissed her, and she closed her eyes. She was back on the beach at Ocean City in her two-piece suit—not quite a bikini—and she was twenty, and he was twenty-one, and they were on their first big adventure together. He was kissing her, and the sand from his hands coated her face and then his sweet lips and then hers. She felt his cushiony body against hers, already comfortable, as if G-d had cut her from his side, then fit them back together.

She opened her eyes, and he asked, "What made you smile?"

"You," she answered. "And the thought of Thrasher fries."

AFTER THEY HAD CONSUMED A BUCKET OF FRIES reheated in their oven, and before the children and the spouses and the grandchildren returned for movie night, Becky and Barry cocooned themselves in the afghan her mother had crocheted for them decades ago, inhaling their life together imbedded in every wool fiber. Satiated by their indulgence, they fell asleep on the sofa, head touching head, as they did so often on Saturday night. That's how Allison found them when she returned with her husband and children and a grocery tote loaded with organic vegetables. "I smell fries!" she said to her husband. "He gave her fries! Why am I even bothering?"

"It's their life, Allison," he replied.

Becky, roused by the sharpness of her daughter's voice, kept her eyes closed but poked Barry in the rib. He poked her back, as if to say, "Ssh." In their shared charade, they listened to Allison analyzing their recklessness. "Early Alzheimer's," she called it. Becky was shocked at how quickly she and Barry had become the ones to be cared for, rather than the ones doing the caring. When she could take it no longer, she thrust the afghan aside, opened her eyes, and announced with as much force as she could muster, "Yes, it's our life, Allison."

"You sneaky eavesdropper!" Allison shouted. "I'm only trying to do my best for you, Mom."

"We know," said Barry, sitting up straight and stretching. "But...."

"But it's her choice," Allison finished in her all-knowing way.

Later they all gathered—the two daughters with their spouses, the five grandchildren, and Andrew—and Jayme put in the DVD of *Fiddler on the Roof*, a film they had watched together so many times as a family. As the film family gathered for the Sabbath, Becky floated above her real family, admiring the prickly love they felt for one another, more invigorating than the saccharine cinematic love. In the shadowy corner of the living room, near the étagère, she saw a gray-haired man tapping his knee impatiently, as if he were waiting for her full attention. She recognized the nervous tapping as a gesture Rabbi Finkelstein had used during the long congregational board meetings, when he had endured enough of his whining congregants. Ezra's jowls were wobbling, and puffiness eclipsed his once exotic eyes.

"So?" he demanded. "When are we going to finish our conversation? It's late."

"There's nothing for us to talk about. What's done is done," Becky replied to the apparition.

"I asked for your forgiveness, Rebecca, my special friend. Are you denying me that forgiveness on your deathbed? Even G-d forgives."

"It is not for me to forgive. You did nothing that I didn't welcome."

"Then have you asked forgiveness of us both from your husband?"

She shuddered. "Who are you to direct my life? Since when am I your spokesman to my husband? Go back where you belong."

"I belong many places, dear Rebecca. And one of them is in your heart." He laughed dryly.

"Not so!" she insisted. But she knew that the first cell in her heart that had now multiplied and exploded until it throttled her ability to breathe had a name, and its name was Rabbi Ezra Finkelstein. She pounded her heart in a two-fisted distortion of the Yom Kippur confessional. "Go. Go. Go," she shouted.

With each cry, Rabbi Finkelstein faded away until all she could see were two beady eyes. Then the eyes were replaced by the worried faces of her husband and children and grandchildren, and his dry laughter by their cacophonous sounds of alarm.

"Mom, mom, what's happening? Mom, do you hear me?"

"She wants us to let her alone. Get the kids out of here. They don't need to see this."

"Nana, why are you crying?"

"Beck, calm down. I'm here. I'm here." A familiar hand stroked her face until her eyes closed and she drifted asleep.

THE NEXT MORNING, AFTER THE HOSPICE NURSE HAD adjusted the narcotics dosage and verified oxygen levels, after the hallucinations of the previous night no longer haunted her, Becky asked Barry to roll her to the lake. The first frost of the season lingered on windshields, but the sun, unimpeded by clouds, warmed her face. They rolled past her neighbor's petrifying chrysanthemums as the wheelchair crunched the blanket of leaves already shed by the first trees beginning their winter rest.

A recently widowed neighbor in her fifties, who had lived on their street for a decade, paused her dog-walking to chat. "Becky, I'm making you a casserole for dinner. Glad to see you out and about." Becky studied her fit figure in her velour jogging suit. She was vigorous enough to start again, but mature enough to understand loss. A good companion for Barry after the rawness of his grieving subsided, Becky thought.

"Nope," Barry said, reading her mind. "Don't even talk about it. I'm a one-girl guy."

But who would he talk to at night in a half-filled bed? And what comfort would he find when he awoke to only the hum of the heater? The lake shimmered in the morning light, capturing the two of them in one image. She in her blue fleece jacket and leather gloves, tubes tethering her to an oxygen tank on the wheelchair. He in his charcoal Tommy Hilfiger jacket she had bought him last Channukah, his hands massaging her shoulders. No Rabbi Finkelstein. A whoosh from above signaled a flock of birds picking up their strays to head south for the winter.

"Now," she told herself. "Now is the time." She arched her face upward to the cloudless sky, seeking strength from whatever lived beyond the azure sky and the circling birds. She turned to Barry and formed the words, "I'm sorry." But no sounds emerged. A vacuum sucked her from her chair. Frantic, she reached for Barry, but her arms stretched out and flapped like the wings of a migrating bird. Her tubes, set free, fluttered in the breeze.

Again she struggled to form the words "I'm sorry," but she was far above the man in the lake, so far away that even if she shouted, her words would sound like the cawing of a crow. Into the eternal blueness she flew with her unspoken confession.

Ferry Man

M ike felt unsettled sitting on the wooden pew in the second row of St. Peters Episcopal Church. He was waiting for the funeral of Big Jim, a man who'd anchored him when he was in high school. And he was sitting behind Big Jim's daughter, the girl he'd loved and never married. He'd done his best to get ready for the funeral—ironed his dress shirt, sewed the button on his blue sports coat, gotten a haircut to minimize the gray strands invading his curly hair. But he could do nothing to fully prepare for this encounter with his twin losses.

Mike longed for movement beneath his feet to settle him down. He missed the vibration of the ferry and its gentle rocking and the slosh of the Potomac River as he piloted it from White's Ferry over to Leesburg—three round trips an hour, eight hours a day, for going on twelve years. To calm himself, Mike studied Mo's neck. When he first touched her neck, it had been buried under a cape of blonde hair, long-since cut, cornsilk hair like that of her daughter Zoe. He remembered being surprised by the softness of Mo's skin on her newly exposed neck and the small mole near the base—not an imperfection but a punctuation to her beauty. He had last touched her neck twenty years ago, the night of senior prom when they made love in the field near White's Ferry. The next day Mo had said, "Last night was a mistake. I like you, Mike. You're my best friend. But we're never going to be anything more." Then she had made her face real serious, like Big Jim did sometimes, and said, "So it's best to break up now. Before college and all that."

Mike watched Mo as Reverend Pullman spoke of Big Jim's great loves—the Orioles, Mo, and of course, his granddaughter Zoe. He could tell from the upward tilt of Mo's head that no stray tear dared wander down her cheek.

"What've you got against crying?" Mike had asked Mo when she didn't get the lead in the musical senior year. They were working in the prop room where the smell of paint, sawdust, and make-believe made him want her.

"It's a waste of energy," she had said, then laughed as if losing the part was no big deal. He had loved her for that strength.

Unlike Mo, Mike cried, though not often. He cried when his father left and he had to juggle working the farm with finishing high school. Cried when his mom was hospitalized with an appendectomy and he thought she might die. Cried when Mo told him they were over. But he learned how to cry where people couldn't see him. He discovered that if he bit the inside of his right cheek, he could hold off the tears until he went out to the field alone where he let them loose as he plowed. Since he'd gotten the ferry job, he'd save the tears for when it was just him, the empty ferry, and the river.

He watched Mo stand, thrust her shoulders back like some kind of drill sergeant, and walk to the pulpit. Her blonde hair had faded and turned strawlike. She sucked her lips inward, then released them as she said, "We all have our Big Jim stories, every single person here." Maybe her sucking action pushed her tears back into her tear ducts and up into her brain where they froze as icicles.

Mike wished he could tell his story about Big Jim treating him to a senior yearbook because the farm wasn't doing well and later teaching him how to drink without getting wasted after Mo dumped him. But Mo hadn't invited him to speak, not that he'd expected her to. Instead, Mike rested in Mo's voice, not bothering to listen to her words. He rarely heard her voice anymore unless she was sitting at the bar at Bassett's after work. When he heard her deep laugh at the other end of the bar, he stopped breathing for a second, then exhaled. As for her Mt. Rushmore face, he knew it like he knew every rock on the shorelines of the river, and though he watched from afar, he knew the comings and goings of her life as well as he knew his small swatch of the Potomac.

After the burial at Heaven's Gate Cemetery as the cluster of people around the grave broke up, Mike made his way toward Mo, who was standing with Zoe, watching the backhoe smother Big Jim's casket. "Mo, I'm so sorry," Mike said, wanting to hug her but not wanting her to stiffen at his touch.

"He loved you, you know," she said, then brushed her hand against his in a perfunctory thank-you.

"Oh, Mike, what am I going to do without grandpa?" Zoe was flinging her arms around his neck, nestling her head in his chest, and sobbing for all three of them. As she leaned into him, he felt a small bump where her stomach should have been flat. So the rumors were true. Zoe was pregnant. At nineteen. Probably to that high-tech guy, the newcomer who'd hung around the ferry store where she'd worked for a while. They said he'd suddenly sold his fancy house and left Poolesville with his family. Mo would have her hands full managing everything, including a new baby, with Big Jim gone and her mother buried not long before.

"I'm always here, Zoe," he said, meaning the words for Mo, too. But Mo had moved away and was studying the headstone of her mother's grave.

ON MONDAY AFTER THE LAST FERRY RUN, MIKE STOPPED by Mo's house with an apple pie just out of the oven, baked by his mother. Mo's car parked on the gravel next to the old pickup signaled that she and the girl were both home, a good time to stop by without Mo feeling encroached upon. The lingering warmth of the pie pan in his chapped hands gave him courage as he rang the bell. The kitchen table overflowed with biscuits, coffee cakes, and foil-wrapped casseroles with barely space for his offering. Mo stacked the two casseroles, making a cove for Mike's pie, then gestured toward the living room. It felt almost right when the three of them sat on the overstuffed furniture, until he glimpsed Big Jim's empty recliner and the lonely oxygen tank in the corner.

Looking at Zoe with her loose top and her slightly puffed face, Mike saw Mo as she'd been when he'd learned she was expecting. Mo's choice had already been made before they talked. She would have the baby. Instead of college, she would stay home with her parents and find a job. "The responsible thing to do," she said. For years Mo had talked about going to college and getting free of the claustrophobia of Poolesville for good.

"I want to marry you," he'd said. "I'm not even asking if the baby is mine. I don't care. I'll take care of you both."

"No," she said. "It's not yours."

"Will you marry the father?"

"No," she said. "It wouldn't work. Besides, he's gone."

She was eighteen when she had shut him out.

"I guess you've heard about the baby." Now it was Zoe talking, her legs curled up under her on the sofa next to Mike. She flicked her hair behind her ears and flipped it on top of her head as if it made her somehow older, more in charge of what was happening. Mike nodded.

"I figured you had. Stuff like that goes viral pretty fast. I'm dropping my college classes, too tired for that and work."

"We'll do just fine," Mo said, smiling at Zoe, then pursing her lips. But Zoe was crying, so Mike put his arms around her like he'd wanted to hold Mo twenty years ago. She felt like a little doe in his arms.

"It's not just fine. It's horrible. I thought he loved me, but he didn't."

"I'm here to help, Zoe," he said.

"It's not your problem," Mo said. "Zoe, go to your room and get yourself together. You shouldn't be crying on Mike's shoulder."

"He's my friend from the ferry store. And grandpa's friend. I'll be friends with whoever I want."

As Zoe stomped up the stairs, Mo rose and pushed Mike toward the front door. He gazed up the stairs, wondering who else Zoe had to talk to now that Big Jim was gone. "Thank you for the pie," Mo said as if he were a nobody. "Now you'd better get going." She closed the door. He heard the lock turn as he stood on the porch.

AFTER A SLEEPLESS NIGHT, MIKE FELT HIS STOMACH settle by the third run of the morning as the ferry cut through the river with its regular slosh. He could finally think straight about Mo, the pie, and the sound of her front door locking. It was over. In fact, it had been over twenty years ago, only he'd been too dumb to realize it. The fall after graduation he'd taken a job in North Carolina, then come back eight years later, leaving behind his ex-wife, a sweet girl whose only crime was not being Mo. All for a glimpse of a woman who barely resembled the girl in his daydreams, if that girl had ever really existed.

The wind picked up, adding extra chop to the river. He and the near-empty ferry were approaching the Maryland shoreline to pick up the last stragglers on their morning commute when he glimpsed a girl near the dock excitedly waving at the ferry. A red ski cap was pulled down over her telltale blonde hair that flapped in the breeze. What the hell was the kid doing here so early? He tooted the horn in three loud blasts as he watched her race to the end of the dock, ahead of two waiting cars. He turned off the motor, looped the rope around the post, and signaled to the drivers to offload.

"Mike! Mike!" she shouted, flinging her arms around him as he tried to maintain his professional demeanor.

"Not now, Zoe," he said, as he removed her arms and began onloading the two waiting vehicles and collecting their fares.

"Can I ride with you so we can talk?" she begged as she trailed him up the ferry ramp.

"If you're sure you're up to the chop and the wind in your condition."

"Not a problem. I'm done with all that morning sickness stuff." After a final warning blast for any latecomers, he started up the engine and the ferry began its round trip.

Zoe huddled next to him, wrapping one arm around him to borrow any warmth she could.

"You're not joking, it's cold."

"I warned you, kid." He slid her arm off his waist. "I'm working."

"Oops. Sorry, Mike."

"So what's up? Does your mom know you're here? No, of course, she doesn't or she'd be going crazy."

"She's going crazy anyhow. Like just because grandpa's gone she can control my life—tell me when to go to sleep, what I should eat or drink, who I should talk to." She looked at Mike's face, her eyes watering, maybe from the wind. "Like talking with you," she added.

"Zoe, I'm not worth upsetting her. She's got enough on her plate."

"You mean me?"

"I mean all the stuff after Big Jim's death—the will, the finances, the house, the hole in her heart. Besides I'm going to be moving on real soon." As he spoke the words, he realized for the first time that he'd made an important decision.

"Not you, too? Then I'll have no one to talk to. No one who understands how she really is, like you do. You're the only one in town who's even trying to understand me." She leaned over and kissed him on the cheek. "Your beard tickles," she giggled, then kissed him again for good measure. "Do you love me, Mike?"

"Of course. You're Big Jim's special girl. But I'm not going to get between you and your mom," Mike said as he tapped the top of her ski cap and laughed. "She's a tough cookie. Besides, I don't have Big Jim's pull with her."

"Oh, I don't want you to be Big Jim. No one can take his place."

Mike felt her hand slip hesitantly down his jacket, then slide into his back jeans pocket and rub up and down his butt. "Girl, are you insane? I'm too old for you. I'm as old as your mom."

"You're not too old. My baby daddy is older than you. Besides, I got tired of the college boys. Too shallow. No sense of the world like you. And their eyes don't catch the sun like yours do."

"It isn't going to happen, Zoe. I'm heading out of here in a couple weeks, as soon as I can line up a place to stay where there are good jobs. I'm just a friend of Big Jim, a high school buddy of your mom, someone you worked with for a couple months. You've got to think about your baby and the rest of your life. Not get yourself messed up with another man who's made a mess of his own life." Then he hustled over to the engine, leaving Zoe alone at the railing while he pretended to study a humming motor that needed absolutely no attention.

HER TEXT "URGENT. MEET AT BASSETTS 7PM" LEFT HIM no choice even though he had lots of packing still to do. He'd given his resignation at the ferry store after his last run, told his mom and brother of his accelerated plans to leave the farm, and called a buddy in Leesburg to line up a place to stay. But once again Mo was messing with his life. When he walked into the restaurant, the piped-in music blared the latest Brad Paisley song. He saw her behind the half-empty bar, sitting in a corner booth, already downing a beer. She lifted her eyes to acknowledge his presence as he slid into the opposite corner of the booth, unzipped his jacket, and began tapping his fingers impatiently on the table.

"Now what?" he asked.

Her red nose and pink-ringed eyes suggested that she'd developed a full-blown cold since yesterday. Or had her brain icicles started leaking?

"Your text? What's so urgent?"

"Zoe," she said. "She's spinning out of control."

"I can see that bigtime. So what do you want from me?"

Mo took a crumpled tissue from her pocket, blotted her eyes, and blew her nose. He bit the inside of his cheek so as not to feel her rare moment of vulnerability.

"She's yours," she said.

"Nope. Don't want a pregnant teenage girlfriend. She's your problem."

"No. I mean she's your daughter."

"What kind of crap are you pulling on me now?" He knew his voice had jumped to football game volume. He rose, leaning across the Formica table to grab her shoulders, shouting, "What in the hell do you mean she's my daughter?"

"She's yours. I lied. She's yours, Mike."

"What the f---? For twenty years you've destroyed two lives. Why should I believe you now?"

"Three lives—all three of ours. And she's yours because there was no one else that summer. Boys I dated and did things with, but no one else I had sex with. She can only be yours. She loves like you loved me, throws her whole self into it. Don't you see it?"

"I got to get outta here." Mike was headed for the door, knowing that the bartender and the customers were busy texting what they'd heard to their friends so that by 8 p.m. all of Poolesville would know. Mo was running after him out the front door, dragging her ratty jacket and purse.

"Don't go in the back. She's out there. Waiting in my car in the parking lot. She can't see you like this."

"You told her? Before you even told me? Who else knows?"

"Big Jim wanted it to be you, sometimes acted like it was, even though I insisted her father was someone else who'd come and gone."

"Crap, Mo. Why didn't you tell me? You've had a thousand chances to tell me."

"I was stupid. I thought I was making your life better, that we'd both make a mistake if I told you, that you'd insist on marrying me or paying child support, that it would screw up the rest of your life. You were my friend, and I did something stupid. But it seemed like the right thing. Until I came home from work today and she said she was falling in love with you, and I freaked out."

Her hands were shaking, and red blotches were taking over her face. He bit the inside of his cheek harder.

"I'm sorry," she said.

"Oh, you're sorry. Twenty years of my life. Nineteen years of keeping me from knowing my daughter. A lifetime of screwing up that girl so she can't tell up from down. Sorry doesn't begin to say it."

"I was wrong. I know it now."

"Crap, you've got lousy timing. Until yesterday I thought I still loved you. Now I've got a new life ahead of me somewhere else. I'm finally unstuck, and now you're sorry."

His stomach, which had settled during the ferry runs, roiled with a chop, chop, chop like the wind on the river. He leaned over and puked on the shrubs. When he was done, he felt her hand stroking his back, the first time she'd really touched him since that night. He heard her whisper, "If it makes you feel any better, I did the same thing at home after she told me about falling in love with you." She handed him some tissues and helped him wipe his face and his shirt. "She wants to talk with you. Are you up to it?"

"Not tonight. I need to pack. Tell her to meet me tomorrow at the 8 a.m. ferry before I leave for Leesburg."

"I'm not asking you to forgive me, as if you could. I'm here for Zoe." Mo helped him to his car, and he could feel her lying eyes on him as he drove down Route 107.

THE BRIGHTNESS OF THE SUN SURPRISED MIKE. AFTER Big Jim's funeral, three days of late fall grayness, and a sleepless night caused by Mo's announcement, he'd expected the sky to match his mood. His brother helped him load cardboard boxes of clothes and his new X-Box into his car. He'd come back later for the rest after he got a place of his own. His mom squeezed him and smoothed his hair like he was thirteen.

"It's time," she said.

"Long past time," his brother added.

He hadn't told them yet about Zoe, afraid they'd complicate his decision. Besides he didn't know whether to believe Mo's announcement. It seemed all too convenient turning him into a father when raising Zoe became a peck of trouble. Yet why would she lie if it meant confessing an even more devastating lie?

He'd agreed to meet the girl at the ferry, knowing there wouldn't be time for much talk. He liked Zoe, had always liked her spunk, her open smile—though she'd been mostly on the outskirts of his life. When she was littler, she'd run around at St. Peters while he talked with Big Jim or tagged along when he and Big Jim went to an Orioles game at Camden Yards. He'd seen more of her for the couple months she worked at the ferry store and had enjoyed giving her free rides when the ferry was nearly empty and her shift had ended. She put sparks in his life. But that was all. If he was hurting, the girl must be hurting a thousand times over, thinking about how every day of her life with Mo had been built on a lie that her father was some unknown guy just passing through, knowing that in a moment of great loneliness, she'd come on to a man who now was supposedly her father. What in the hell should she do, could she do, with all this new information?

He passed Poolesville High, followed the turn in 107 past St. Peters, and a half mile later slowed down at the field near the ferry store where he and Mo had laid after the senior prom, serenaded by crickets and owls. Then two best friends, buzzed from beer and the final glow of high school, had made love on the damp grass, and everything had changed. What if he embraced Zoe as his own on faith? He'd finally yanked Mo from his heart, and now she would return to his life forever. Could he ever move on?

As he pulled up to the dock, first in line, he saw no signs of Zoe or the pickup truck. In ten minutes the ferry would return to Poolesville, and his replacement would let down the ramp and onload Mike for the next phase of his life. The ferry drew closer as cars queued up, and the new ferry man tooted an extra-long blast to hurry along people lingering over coffee in the ferry store. No sign of Zoe. She was a sharp kid. Probably decided not to get riled up over Mo's act of desperation. Or maybe she was hiding in embarrassment over yesterday.

"Hey, Mike, off to better places?" his replacement called out as he waved Mike onto the ramp.

"Off to my future," Mike shouted back.

As the ferry filled, Mike got out of his car and stared into the sun, wondering if maybe Zoe had come after all and was trapped behind the growing line of cars. She should have gotten here fifteen minutes ago if she'd wanted to talk. He heard the clank of the gate closing and the startup burp of the engine, then felt the soft jolt as the ferry began its trip across the Potomac. Over the engine hum, he though he heard someone calling his name. Shielding his eyes from the sun, he spotted a bobbing red ski cap and hands waving frantically.

"Mike!" His name traveled across the river. Or had he just imagined the sound and the bobbing ski cap? He turned away from the sun and focused on the Leesburg shoreline and the possibilities beyond the trees.

Mid-river his cell vibrated. He pulled it out and read, "Sorry. Late. Angry?"

"Not at you," he wrote.

"Sad?"

"Yes."

"Happy?"

He paused, feeling the familiar rocking of the ferry, looking at his car stuffed with boxes. He tried to make her out standing by the dock as if seeing her would answer the question. But all he could see now was a red dot.

"Yes," he tapped quickly before the red dot disappeared. "I'm angry and sad and happy." He bit the inside of his cheek, but the tears came anyway. Then his replacement tooted the horn, and the ferry glided into the Leesburg dock.

Wading in the Water

When Elsie pulled Mo from the Potomac River, the water and muck had infiltrated Mo's jeans jacket and filled her yellow rain boots, making her much heavier than her 115 pounds. Elsie had never lugged anything this unwieldy. Even an overturned canoe left by a careless renter was easier to manage. Mo's eyes were closed, her skin beneath the mud a soft shade of violet, her lips an intense blue, her breath nonexistent.

"Come on, girl!" Elsie yelled as she scooped debris out of Mo's mouth, tore open the jacket and a flimsy blouse, and began pounding the woman's chest. "Somebody help!" she shouted in the direction of the ferry dock, knowing full well that the ferry was way on the other side of the Potomac. Elsie pressed her lips against Mo's blue lips and breathed all she had into the woman again and again. Hearing no response, Elsie beat her arthritic hands on the bare chest of a woman who had no right to die. "You gotta make it, Maureen. Come on now, breathe."

When a small breath escaped followed by a gag and an expulsion of water, Elsie let out a whoop. Mo's eyelids flickered open. She squinted as if she expected someone other than Elsie staring down at her. "Shit. Where's Zoe?"

Mo closed her eyes as if willing herself back into the river. By the time she opened them again, Elsie had pulled her up to the grass field next to the ferry store and plopped down next to the water-logged woman, panting from the exertion. "Good thing I was at the store this morning getting ready for spring opening," Elsie was muttering to the prone body. She paused long enough to catch her breath and added, "I looked outta my window and there you were, just beyond the shore, getting out of a pickup and parading into the river like you could walk yourself the whole way from Maryland to Virginia. And I said, Elsie, something ain't right here. But who woulda known it was Big Jim's girl?"

"Can you be quiet? My head's pounding." Mo turned her head in the direction of the river.

Elsie leaned next to Mo's mouth and took a big sniff. "Just as I thought. You've been drinking."

"Shut up."

Elsie peered up Route 107, hoping a car was headed to the ferry, even though it was mid-morning in early April, a time when few had need to cross the river. Without help, she could never get Mo up the stairs to Elsie's apartment above the ferry store, and Mo was starting to shiver fiercely in the breeze off the river. But Route 107 was quiet.

"Put your arms around my neck," she ordered.

Mo raised her arms limply a few inches above the grass, then dropped them as if the exertion had taken all that was left in her. Elsie crouched down and stripped Mo of her jacket and boots and soggy pants. Ignoring the pain in her bum knee, she slung Mo over her right shoulder, balancing Mo's head and shoulders with the lower part of her torso. "Upsie daisy, girl. We're taking a trip."

There'd been enough dying in that family to last a decade, Elsie thought. Martha about eighteen months ago, then less than a year later, Big Jim. She'd be damned if she'd let another Shockley pass away too soon. Like a mother lifting a truck that was crushing her baby, Elsie dragged Mo to the ferry store steps, rested just long enough to stop her heart from popping out of her chest, and bounced her friends' daughter step by step up the stairs to the apartment.

ELSIE SPOKE SOFTLY ON THE PHONE TO DOC PIKE, keeping one eye on the bedroom where Mo lay propped up on two feather pillows and buried under every stale quilt and blanket Elsie could find.

"Keep filling her with warm coffee. I'll be by to check her out soon as my schedule lets up. Unless you want to call 911 and get her taken to the hospital now," he told her.

"No need for that. There'll be enough gossip as it is. I think you and I can get her through this." A soft moan, like a baby lamb bellyaching, came from the bedroom. "Gotta go, Doc. My patient calls." Elsie went into the kitchen and made some coffee like Zoe used to in the ferry store.

"Here I am, Maureen," she announced as she handed Mo a mug with a picture of old Poolesville. "Got you some nice hot coffee, same as we sell in the store."

"I've got to get across the river," Mo said. Her hand knocked the mug aside, spilling coffee on the bedspread, hand-embroidered by Elsie's long-deceased aunt for a marriage that never materialized. "Oh, shit. I didn't mean to do that."

Elsie blotted the spill with a tea towel. "Don't you worry, Maureen. That quilt's seen better days," she said as she coaxed the fluid into Mo until her skin started to pink up and her shaking became an occasional shudder. Elsie folded her arms around Mo and rocked her like she knew Martha and Big Jim would have, humming a melody from the hymnal at St. Peters. Underneath the smell of fresh soap and shampoo, Elsie still sniffed the muck of the river in Mo's hair.

"I've got to get across the river. Now," Mo announced as she untangled herself from Elsie's arms.

"You ain't going anywhere now, girl," Elsie said. "Unless you want me to call 911 to get you a ride to the hospital." She stood and marched across the bedroom, blocking the door with her wide-beamed body.

"So I'm in prison here. That's how you want to play it. You're going to stand there like some kind of guard keeping me from crossing the river to Zoe."

"Exactly. Now if you'd tried using the ferry instead of wading in the water like a damn fool, I'd say go right ahead—cross that river and see your daughter. But your head's not working right. Too much alcohol and too much sadness." Elsie pushed her dresser in front of the door to create another more stable barrier, just in case Mo's anger gave her the strength to push Elsie aside.

"Go to Hell. After all my parents did for you, you old waddling duck. This is how you're repaying them?"

Elsie held back. No sense fueling Mo's anger or letting her mix one messed up life with another. "Now you just rest, Maureen. Put your head back on those pillows and let all that sadness flow on out. Go ahead. No shame in crying once in a while."

"I hate you. I hate this damn town. Everybody butts in when they should be taking care of their own affairs. Who are you to give me permission to cry?"

"I'm just saying it's easier sometimes to just let go and clean yourself out."

"See. That shows you how little you know. I've cried enough when no one was looking. When Zoe left me to live with her father and when she told me second-hand that she never wanted to see me or talk to me again. No, I'm not staying here with an old lady telling me to go ahead and cry when I should be crossing the river to see my grand...." Mo caught herself, then studied Elsie's face.

Elsie pursed her lips, then manufactured a surprised look. "Well, congratulations. So you've got yourself a grand-daughter."

"See. You already knew. It only happened last night, and already the ferry store manager and probably every other person in this horrible place knows my private business."

"Don't you go blaming Poolesville for your sadness." Elsie stopped because Mo knew her sins, sure as Elsie knew her own. No need for reminding. But it was too late. Mo was flinging off the quilts and leaping from the bed. Elsie's flannel nightgown flapped over Mo's skinny body as she raced toward the bedroom door and threw her weight against Elsie like she was trying to move a boulder. But Elsie, who had long ago learned how to stand her ground, wrapped her arms around the flailing woman and pinned her against the wall, humming again the hymn they both knew so well.

LATER, AFTER DOC PIKE'S SEDATIVE HAD SETTLED MO down, Elsie pulled an armchair into the bedroom and propped her leg with the swollen knee on the foot of the bed. Mo was snoring like Big Jim used to when he rested in his recliner after a Sunday dinner. Elsie remembered washing dishes in the kitchen with Martha and slipping into girl talk as if Martha and Jim's marriage had never disrupted their high school friendship. Elsie couldn't figure out which one of them she had loved the most and who was most to blame for turning the trio into a couple.

Mo looked so pretty now. She had Martha's turned up little nose and Martha's heart-shaped lips. Usually you couldn't see Martha in Mo because she had so much fight in her face. But looking at her now, Elsie could scarcely believe she was old enough to have a granddaughter, and Zoe a mother herself, despite Elsie's efforts to keep her away from that married man who had no business coming on to a teenager.

Big Jim would have known what to do with this mess. He'd always kept things together. He would have just picked up the phone and called Zoe and told her, get over it, girl. Your mom has done some horrible things, kept secrets she shouldn't have. But she's always loved you and taken care of you. So just talk to her once in a while and let her see her grandbaby. But Big Jim was gone, not long after Martha got breast cancer and died. He gave in to pneumonia almost like he wanted it to take him. Now there was no one left who had his pull over Zoe.

Maureen—such a pretty name, especially how Big Jim stretched out the "e" sound so you could feel every ounce of his love for his beautiful daughter. Almost everyone but Martha and Big Jim called the girl "Mo." It fit her more than the delicate "Maur-eeeen." But she was Maur-eeeen now, lying there so gentle, so pretty, filling Elsie's bedroom with young life so that Elsie didn't even notice the water stain on the ceiling or the wallpaper pulling away near the closet door. Maur-eeeen. Prettier than Martha when she was wasting away in bed as Elsie fed her chicken broth and wondered if Big Jim would turn to Elsie when Martha died. She hated herself for ogling the remains of her friend's life, imagining what it would feel like if he turned to her when grief overtook him. She hated Martha for dying. She hated them both for leaving her here alone to miss them.

The thumping from the kitchen signaled that the drier was working extra hard to dry Mo's water-logged clothes. Mo would need something hopeful to look at when she awoke. Maybe the daffodils in the flower garden near the shed. Elsie lifted Mo's hand to test her consciousness, and when all she heard was a soft mmm, she tied Mo's hands together with the sash from a bathrobe, just in case Mo woke up with some crazy idea before she'd gotten the alcohol out of her system. "Wh…?" Mo muttered, then drifted away again, her hands bound together in a prayer.

Elsie slipped the remaining sedatives into her pocket, tiptoed from the bedroom, put on her wind-breaker, and walked down to the garden. As she waddled over the uneven ground toward the canoe shed, she realized Mo was right. She did walk like a duck. Had Big Jim and Martha seen her like some pitiable creature who needed a meal every once and again? It hadn't seemed that way then. The laughter and gossip had flowed easily. But maybe it was just their Christian charity, nothing more. Or maybe the duck waddle business was just Mo being Mo.

Elsie bent over to clip the daffodils from their roots, listening for footsteps on the stairs in case her fugitive attempted another escape. The stunted daffodils looked worn out, their yellow pale as chicken broth. Some of the stems hadn't even blossomed. Had she neglected to work enough top soil around the bulbs? Had the unforgiving clay beneath the top soil restricted the bulbs? Elsie set the daffodils on the grass and dragged the bag of top soil from the shed along with a trowel. She clawed at the clay beneath the top soil to loosen it, then dumped more rich, dark top soil on the chunks. She plunged both hands into the soil between the plants and kneaded it. Maybe it was too late to make a difference for the daffodils, but she could get the soil ready for the planting of the May annuals.

As the ferry tooted, announcing its arrival for the 5 o'clock crossing, she saw Martha and Big Jim hiding back behind the shed. She was with them. The three of them, no more than sixteen, were sharing a cigarette and a beer. Big Jim had wedged himself between the two girls, Martha's head on his right shoulder, Elsie's on his left, though he was listing slightly to the right. The smell of the forbidden beer intoxicated her, or was she light-headed because of the taste of the shared cigarette and the warmth of Jim's body beneath his baseball uniform?

"I'm taking care of Maureen for you," Elsie told them. "Don't you worry."

She plunged her hands once more into the soil. As she crushed some lingering clay clods, she heard feet clumping down the stairs and turned. "Maureen! Where do you think you're going?"

Mo grabbed the bottom of the handrail, the sound of her name almost knocking her off her feet. Beneath her disheveled hair, her frozen face made Elsie's jaw ache.

"Gotta run, Elsie. The ten-minute warning just sounded. Thanks for everything." She began sprinting across the field toward the ferry store's gravel lot.

Elsie rearranged her body so she could stand without further irritating her bum knee. Limping across the field after Mo, she called out, "Wait. You can't go. You aren't up to it. Look how your balance is all off. You've got enough drugs and drink left in you to put a horse to sleep."

But Mo wasn't listening. She had reached Big Jim's pickup and was fumbling around on the gravel, looking for something.

"See what I mean. Can't even find your keys. Come on back up, Mo. Let me feed you some dinner and then you can spend the night and finish sleeping it off. Wait for tomorrow. You're going to drive off the road in that condition."

"I can't wait. Zoe needs me. She's all alone with a baby and her clueless father. Who's going to help her if the milk doesn't come in right? Who's going to show her how to soothe a crying baby? She needs her mother. Ah, there they are." She was waving a key ring triumphantly in the air.

The ferry tooted two blasts. "Hey, John. Hold the ferry. I'm coming," she shouted toward the new ferry man who had just finished loading the lone car for the river crossing.

"You tried to walk your way across the river because of your Zoe craziness and almost drowned, and now you think Zoe'll open the door to you and let you in just like that. You fool."

But Mo was in the driver's seat of the pickup and slamming the door.

"Maureen, I promised Big Jim and Martha I'd take care of you. Don't make me a liar!" Elsie threw herself on the hood and pounded it to get Mo's attention over the racing engine. The pickup zipped backward, dumping Elsie to the ground and leaving her with gravel burns on her arms and legs. "Stop," she called to the pickup barreling toward the dock slightly off kilter. "Stop. Oh Jesus, stop," she pleaded as the truck missed the dock and slid into the Potomac.

From the gravel lot, Elsie watched breathless as John jumped into the river, yanked the pickup door open, and pulled a woman in a jeans jacket and yellow boots onto the dock. As the pickup continued to fill with water, John lifted the woman and she leaned into his chest and draped her arms around his neck like an Easter tableau.

No need to call out again, Elsie thought, jutting out her jaw as protection. No need for the stunted daffodils in the bedroom. Maureen has found someone else to do the saving, and I've got her bed linens to wash.

Substitutes

ithin ten minutes of Jamal's arrival, the dining room chairs were turned on their side, the crystal bowl Ericka brought from Berlin trembled twice, and a crumb trail linked sugar cookies on the kitchen island to Jamal's hiding place under the table.

"Jamal, please come out from under that table," Ericka said, summoning the kindest voice from her stern repertoire so as not to scare off her new charge.

"It's my fort. I can't come out. They'll attack me." He yanked a crumbling cookie from his pocket, stuffed it into his mouth for nourishment, then stretched his right arm and held it like a rifle. "Bam…bam…bam. Gotcha."

"Your room, Jamal, let's go see your room. I've readied it for you. I promise you no one will shoot if you come with me." She leaned over and rubbed his tight black curls, but the boy flinched and scowled at her best attempt at a smile.

"No way. I'm in charge. Can't come in."

She wondered why she had bothered to straighten up the house for the boy's arrival. Who was she trying to impress? Would Mrs. Lindwell have taken Jamal with her if the sofa cushions were flat or dust coated the end tables?

"Come," she said to the boy, this time using the no-nonsense voice she inherited from her German mother. "Upstairs. Unpack." Then she switched back to her softer voice, "And a surprise is waiting for you on your bed, something Mrs. Lindwell said you'd like." Jamal emerged from beneath the table, pushing aside a chair, and streaked up the stairs before she could show him the way.

"It's the second room on the right, Jamal," she called, afraid that he might enter her bedroom by mistake and destroy it before she even reached the upstairs hall. "Wait for me. Don't open the gift yet." Her left hip, which had succumbed to arthritis far too soon, slowed her as she negotiated the steps. Already she heard paper ripping and cardboard tearing and Jamal shouting, "Star Wars! A Star Wars light sabre!" Then the rhythmic bouncing of mattress springs, delighted yelps, and the crash of something hitting the floor.

By the time Ericka reached the door of Jamal's temporary bedroom, Jamal was wedged under the bed, far away from the jagged pieces of what used to be the new football lamp. "I told you to wait. Look what happens when you don't listen," she said. "That lamp I bought just for you. Hard-earned money. Nobody gives me that money. Now it is a waste, just like garbage."

A light sabre poked out from under the bed and angled in her direction. "Bam...bam...bam," he said. "Gotcha."

"He won't eat vegetables, spits them out or makes a mountain of them on the side of his plate. Sometimes I let him go to school with that sweaty dog smell because I'm too tired to fight him to take a bath. And yesterday his teacher called from the summer reading readiness program to say he's having trouble reading. They think it's his eyes. All day, he walks around the room at will, running his fingers along the chalkboard, poking other children in the back. This week has felt like a year."

Ericka was sitting across the kitchen table from Louise, her best friend from work. It was Saturday, which meant twenty-four hours today with Jamal, followed by another twenty-four hours tomorrow, interrupted only by his sleep, and even then he awakened crying. To get the energy out of his system, she had shooed him outdoors with his light sabre where no harm could be done to the large oak tree in the backyard or the picnic table. Louise patted her friend's hand, sipped her coffee, and inhaled the coffee fragrance, common stalling tactics that Ericka recognized from staff meetings. Louise was not one to rush into anything and had, in fact, urged Ericka to think twice before taking in a foster child.

"I know. You're going to say, give it time," Ericka pre-empted her.

"So give it time then. Didn't Mrs. Lindwell warn you at the placement interview that there's a period of adjustment?"

"But who knew the reality? Living this is very different from imagining a boy who needs kindness and attention. This feels like payback." She waited for Louise to say something, but Louise only shook her head. One week with Jamal had replaced Ericka's tentative smile with a permanent frown, deepened her forehead wrinkles, and devastated her almost as much as the loss of her daughter. Long before Jamal was actually here, before she even knew anything about him, she'd invested herself in the idea of him, in having somewhere to put her love now that Bella was gone.

"He's a little boy, Ricki. How bad can a little boy be?" Louise walked behind Ericka and wrapped her arms around her friend. "I'm here for you. And you'll be here for Jamal."

Ericka allowed herself to lean into Louise, relaxing for a few seconds in her friend's fleshy arms and bromides, protected momentarily from her own doubts. It would be all right, it had to be all right, fate had to turn at some point. She imagined Jamal two weeks from now, smelling of soap and shampoo, cuddled next to her on the huge double chair listening to her read from *The Brothers Grimm*, like she used to read to Bella. If she could only hold on for a while, maybe….

"Help! Help!" a familiar voice shrieked from the backyard. "Help me now!"

"Good Lord, it's the boy. He's up the tree," said Louise, peering out the kitchen door.

"Up the tree? Gott im Himmel, how did he get up there?" In seconds the two of them stood at the base of the oak tree, staring at Jamal perched on one of the top branches. With one hand, the boy balanced himself against the trunk as the branch, scarcely thick enough to support him, bobbed twenty feet above the hard soil and the picnic table where his light sabre rested.

"Come get me! I can't get down!" Ericka heard the tears in his voice.

"Your ladder, Ricki?"

"Too short."

"Maybe if we put it on the table, then rest it against the trunk?"

"Too risky. Call 911. Quick. Before the boy falls."

"Get me now!" Jamal inched closer to the trunk and flung his arms around it, but they barely encircled halfway.

"Don't worry, Jamal," Ericka called to the teetering boy. "The fire department will be here soon. Don't move. Be brave like Yoda and Luke Skywalker and Rey and everybody else in Star Wars. Before you know it, you'll be down here with your light sabre."

As Louise rattled off details to 911, Ericka stared helplessly at the tree, particularly at the dark scar stretching four feet from the v-point of the base. She wished now that she'd paid a legitimate tree doctor to prune the tree, not the man in the blue pickup who'd knocked on her door and cut some low-lying branches for fifty dollars, a reasonable fee if you assumed the dark scar didn't suggest a fissure in the tree's core, or if you assumed no human being would trust his life to an upper branch of an ancient tree.

"Cushions," she directed Louise. "Get the sofa cushions. We'll put them under the tree in case...."

Together the two women positioned three floral cushions on the table and three at the likely spot the boy would hit if he fell. As the boy whimpered, Ericka forced herself not to think about how she would clean the upholstery. "You're safe, Jamal. It's soft here. Don't worry." Before she could add, "Just wait a bit longer," the boy leaped from the branch. But his trajectory, interrupted by the leaves and other branches, was not straight downward toward the neatly arranged cushions.

"Jamal!" Ericka shouted as she dashed in his direction and stretched her arms skyward just in time to absorb the force of his fall. Backward she tumbled, her arms cradling his thin body. Backward with nothing but her ample body to protect the boy from the impact of the hard soil. Backward until she hit the ground followed by abdominal pain more searing than childbirth. The boy was sobbing against her chest, each violent sob provoking yet another shooting pain.

"Mommy...mommy," he murmured between a strange choking sound, half hiccup, half gasp. Ericka felt a sticky liquid against her chest and looked down to find blood gushing from the boy's mouth, coating his chin, soaking into her blouse. Had she maimed the child?

Louise gently extricated Jamal from Ericka's grasp, stroked his face, and plunged her fingers into his mouth. "Ssh, Jamal. You'll be fine. It's just a tooth. There's a big space where it used to be. We'll find it somewhere and leave it tonight for the tooth fairy. And you've got a split lip. You must have bit it when you landed. Here, press this pillow hard against your mouth to stop the blood. Hold the cushion tight. Now I'm going to put you down and help Miss Ericka."

By the time Louise situated Jamal and the cushion on the picnic table, the firetruck and an ambulance had arrived. The EMTs tested Ericka's limbs and instructed her to give a number from one to ten that measured the pain, while Jamal whimpered "Mommy" into the cushion. Even in all her pain, Ericka could tell he was trembling.

"Your mommy and you will be going to the hospital," said the EMT as he separated Jamal from the blood-stained cushion and lifted him up. "Leave this old cushion here." In the ambulance, the EMT hooked up Ericka to an IV, and Jamal burrowed next to her as if seeking refuge from the strange sounds and instruments. His lip was temporarily patched, and his tiny hand pressed a gauze pad against the hole where his tooth had once been.

"No worries, my little one. Ouch, don't move so much. Each bump makes me hurt more. And you? Your mouth, is it hurting?"

He shook his head, then whispered, "I want Mommy."

Amidst all this tumult, he was calling out for a woman who rarely fed him, who left him to care for himself while she went who knows where for who knows what—a woman who didn't deserve a child, not even one as willful and troublesome as Jamal. And she, who cooked and cleaned and cared for her daughter, she had been rewarded for doing her duty by Bella's abandonment. The ambulance siren cried out with an urgency that matched Ericka's pain.

"JAMAL, I'VE GOT A SURPRISE FOR YOU."

Louise offered a folded cloth napkin to the boy propped up in Ericka's bed watching a Star Wars marathon on t.v., swallowed by the down pillows and the sky-blue comforter, which contained him long enough for everyone to recover from the day's catastrophe. Ericka lay next to Jamal, dozing on and off while the meds temporarily muffled the throbbing of her cracked ribs.

"Whatcha got? A cookie?" Jamal asked Louise. He leaned forward, accidentally elbowing Ericka as he reached for the cloth.

"Oooh," Ericka mumbled in her half-sleep. "No bouncing."

"Gently, Jamal. Open the napkin carefully and you'll see. Something for you, from you."

He shook the napkin and, flapping it above his head, called out, "You tricked me. There's nothing. Liar!"

"It dropped, Jamal. See there in the folds of the comforter. It's your tooth, the one that came out too soon when you jumped from the tree." Louise plucked the tiny white tooth from the bedding, placed it in the boy's hands, and folded her hands around his.

"Later when we put you to bed, we'll wrap the tooth back in the napkin and put it under your pillow. And in the middle of the night, the tooth fairy will fly into your room to take the tooth and leave you money in exchange."

"That's a silly story. She never came before. Who will tell her I'm not with mommy?" Jamal cupped the tooth in his hands and blew on it, testing its permanence.

"We'll just have to write the tooth fairy a note after I make you and Miss Ericka something soft to eat so we don't hurt those stitches on your lip. Now stay quiet while I'm downstairs in the kitchen and take good care of Miss Ericka. She needs to rest."

As Louise left the room, Jamal turned his attention to Ericka as she exhaled a long, piercing whistle. He laughed, then wiggled her nose to see if it stopped the whistle, which it didn't. Suddenly Ericka's eyes popped open, and she stared at Jamal as if she were expecting Bella and someone had just made a shocking substitution. She studied his bandaged lip and remembered what the ER doctor had said about Jamal's x-ray, the signs of old fractures like someone had whacked him in the nose. She wondered what other scars the boy was carrying. In some crazy naïveté, she had thought that a light sabre and sugar cookies could turn off his anger and make him grateful to live in a tidy house with a football lamp purchased just for him.

"Do you hurt?" she asked.

"Just when I laugh."

Before long the spacecraft hurtled through time and space, taking them away from their pain—if only for a moment. Jamal's eyes drooped, then closed beneath fluttering black lashes, the boy exhausted from sirens that must have dredged up memories of more terrifying sirens in his short life. Ericka felt his body tip into hers, triggering yet another twinge, and she would have prodded him in the other direction, except for his warmth. She pretended that he liked her, that he found comfort in her orderly house, in her nutritious food laid out on the kitchen table, in her body ready to protect his from harm. But she had provided the same to Bella her whole life until the girl spurned it all for a long-haired creep, who introduced her to things a nice girl shouldn't know about. No, to be fair to the creep, as if a concession were due, Bella had turned from her long before he appeared on the scene. Now, the money deducted from Ericka's paycheck for Bella's college even when the washing machine threatened to expire, remained untouched in the bank, waiting. She saw some of Bella in the boy—her willfulness, her daring—qualities that endangered them and horrified Ericka. But unlike Bella, the boy in his stillness revealed vulnerability beneath the recklessness.

"Ah, Jamal, I could love you if you let me," Ericka whispered.

Downstairs she heard talking, probably Louise calling to tell her family she would be spending the night here tending to two invalids. Ericka winced again, the pain harsher this time, a sign the medicine was wearing off.

"Hungry?" Louise entered the bedroom balancing two bowls of chicken noodle soup on a tray.

"Just the boy. Leave his soup here."

"You've got to eat after what you've been through."

Ericka turned her head away, in no mood to be mothered with its implications of incompetency and frailty.

"I heard you downstairs," Ericka said. "Were you on the phone with your kids?"

"No. I called Bella."

"Bella? You know you're not to call her. No one's to call her."

"She has a right to know about you, but no one picked up, so I left a voicemail."

"Not surprised she didn't pick up. She won't call, you know, even if she's not doped up on something. Who needs her? There's nothing to be gained by having her hang around to steal cash from my wallet. Better to be sad than live with that. Now, will you get me my pain med? My ribs are starting to kill me."

Louise shrugged and headed off with the soup. Outside the wind was acting up, and branches from the oak tree tapped like gunshots against Ericka's bedroom window. She wondered if the tree were reminding Jamal of the consequences of invading its territory or warning her of the folly of taking another child into her home.

THE MORNING SUN HAD AWAKENED JAMAL, WHO WAS jumping on Ericka's bed, smacking the picture above her head with each ascension and shocking her ribs with each descent. He was waving a dollar bill and singing, "The tooth fairy came!" But by the time Ericka raised her voice to remind him that her body was still in pain and furniture was not a play toy, Jamal had hopped off the bed and was racing downstairs.

"Hungry! Hungry!" he shouted as he pounded the steps.

A note on the night table said that Louise was running errands. Ericka pushed her body up from the pillows, inched her legs out from the comforter, and dangled them over the side of the bed, breathing shallowly to avoid the sting of deep breaths. Just a couple minutes sitting here should reorient her head to the real world, she told herself, then she'd check on the boy's breakfast. The doorbell was ringing. Probably Louise forgot the house key.

"Jamal," she called downstairs. "Answer the door, please."

But Louise was rarely careless that way. Besides, she wouldn't have noticed the missing key until she'd finished her errands. And it was an ungodly hour for neighbors to stop by, or for young men to sell window replacements or new roofs. The bell was ringing repeatedly, like the person had a right to be inside. Bella. She'd come, probably out of reluctant duty after hearing Louise's message, but still, she'd come. Ah, Bella, at last after a whole year. Well, she wouldn't be getting a warm welcome, Ericka told herself, not after what she'd done. Again, the bell rang, followed by loud, belligerent knocks so like her daughter.

"Get that door, Jamal, and invite her in. I'm moving slow."

She pushed off the bed and shuffled across the room, down the hallway, while downstairs Jamal fumbled with the front door lock, turning it this way and that. From the top of the stairs, she saw the door swing open as Jamal shouted, "What are you doing here?"

"I've come to see Ms. Rogers, Jamal. Can you get her for me?"

Ericka recognized the officious tone of Mrs. Lindwell before she saw the familiar steel hair atop a tall woman. For goodness sakes, she wondered, one of those unannounced visits on a Sunday morning? Didn't the woman have a life besides work?

"She's in bed. She's hurt," Jamal said.

"Right here, Mrs. Lindwell, I'm coming right down." Ericka ran her hands through her hair to restore order, then fussed with her pajama collar and checked that every button was fastened.

"Take your time, Ms. Rogers. Don't hurt yourself anymore by rushing."

When she reached the bottom of the stairs, Jamal lifted his pajama top, drummed his belly, then raced off to the kitchen shouting "Hungry tummy."

"My goodness, Ms. Rogers, I can see you are really having a time of it."

"It's all good. Just a bit early in the morning for everything to be in top shape."

"Oh, I'm talking about yesterday's accident. I can see the boy's in grand form, but you're the one who's taken the brunt of it. What a noble thing you did catching Jamal as he fell, putting your own body in the way to protect him."

"How do you know? Who told you?"

"The hospital. It's protocol. Whenever one of our children comes in for a visit, we are notified at once. The ER doctor was quite effusive about your concern for Jamal."

"He's under my charge. Anyone would have done the same."

"No, not true at all, Ms. Rogers. You are exactly what we look for in our foster parents. Unfortunately, you are in no position to care adequately for Jamal for the next few weeks, maybe longer according to the doctor. So it's best for Jamal, best for you, that we place Jamal with another home. He's barely been here—just eight days—so the attachment can't yet be a big issue. This in no way reflects negatively on you, Ms. Rogers. In fact, as soon as you are healed, we'll put you at the top of our list for another child. I've already put all the details of your heroism into our system. On behalf of the Social Service Department and on behalf of Jamal, we thank you deeply."

Ericka sank onto the cushionless sofa, her legs no longer able to keep her upright.

"Oh, Ms. Rogers, are you okay? I'm sorry I was so blunt. Do you need some water?"

"Just a little light-headed. You've caught me off guard. I mean, can't we work it out? I'm tough. The boy and I have bonded already, and I'd hate for him to think I'm turning him out."

"We'll make sure he understands, but you can see by how you are now and by how energetic Jamal is, that this is no longer a safe fit for either of you."

Why did she feel bereft about a boy who had turned her house and her life into shambles? Less than twenty-four hours ago, she was moaning about how she could endure another day.

"Will I be able to see him, Mrs. Lindwell?"

"It's best for the time being that you not visit his new home. It interferes with the bonding with the new family. But perhaps by Thanksgiving, we can arrange for a visit, and by then, you will be strong enough to have a new child."

As if one child could substitute for another. As if Bella could have ever been replaced by Jamal.

"I can manage. My friend will be back shortly. She'll be helping me for the short-term. Please, Mrs. Lindwell, don't take my child."

"Let's be reasonable. He's a foster child, a visitor you cared for and nurtured for a short while. He is not your child." She squeezed Ericka's hand, then turned toward the kitchen.

"Jamal, let's get dressed and pack up your suitcase. Miss Ericka is hurting so much she can't take care of you right now. I have a wonderful place where they have two little boys about your age to play with and lots of toys and a swing set in the backyard. You will stay there so Miss Ericka can heal."

"But my light sabre?"

"We'll take it with us."

"And the money from the tooth fairy?"

"You can take that, too."

"How will she find me?"

"We'll write a letter to the tooth fairy."

"No, not the tooth fairy. Miss Ericka. How will she know where I am?"

The voices grew softer as Mrs. Lindwell and Jamal climbed the stairs, already an intimacy between them that excluded Ericka. This momentary wrenching he was feeling would become part of Jamal's turbulent history, the split lip blending with the broken nose, one siren blending with another. Would he even remember her name or the puffy blue comforter or the way he nestled next to her and fell asleep?

September 12

Ericka didn't open the letter from the Navy. She knew what was in it. Instead, she let it fester on the dining room table until September 11, the date of the annual memorial service, the same date that seventeen years ago, a flight heading for California was steered into the Pentagon where it crashed and killed Randall Everett Rogers, other military and civilian employees, and everyone on board. As was her ritual, at exactly 9:45 a.m., the time of impact, she took the letter, set it ablaze and watched the flames consume it, as they had consumed Ev's body, removing any visible reminder of who he had been. As the flames flickered and the letter turned to embers, she waited for her release from Ev for the next three hundred sixty-five days.

Except for her daughter Bella, who had become used to seeing the letter burn and had stopped asking questions long before she grew up and disappeared from Ericka's life, nobody else knew about the ritual. Not even her best friend Louise, who knew almost everything about Ericka. And certainly not Ericka's mother, who had lived through worse in Communist Germany and had never been told the full story about Ev.

On September 12, Ericka received a cryptic letter from her mother that brought up the long-buried name of Everett, as Mutter had insisted upon calling him, despite Ericka's repeated requests that he not be mentioned at all. *Meine liebe tochter* the letter began, loving words she had rarely heard from her mother's lips, not even when she said good-bye after her last visit to Berlin, long ago when Bella was just a baby.

Meine liebe tochter,

Today the rain reminds me of the day you left Germany and went with Everett to start a new life in America. It was gray that day, with winds that whipped the rain against the windows of my flat and made me fear for you up so high for so long, traveling across an ocean with no place to land if the weather battered the plane. I was right to fear for you and planes, though I got the date wrong.

Today I remember all of that day you left. How strong and handsome Everett looked in his uniform— full of American self-entitled optimism. And you, liebe tochter, your face flushed with love told me all I needed to know about why you were going to a place so different. I never mentioned my sadness, my fears. It would have been wrong to spoil your happiness, knowing that life itself has a way of spoiling every happiness we find. She will find out soon enough, I told myself.

Today I remember, too, your phone call on September 11, 2001. Your voice trembling, telling me that Everett had died, that you and the little girl were alone, that you were overwhelmed. I knew what you were asking, Ericka. But to fly across the ocean and help raise a toddler in a strange place, that I couldn't do. So I pretended not to hear the unspoken request.

I did wrong, very wrong. We must learn, you and I, to respond to the message beneath the words. And time flies.

Mutter

WHEN LOUISE CAME TO THEIR REGULAR THURSDAY dinner, Ericka was waiting with the letter. "Flowers for my friend," Louise announced as she placed sunflowers in Ericka's outstretched hand. "What's this?" she added as she noticed the letter.

"What does this mean?" Ericka asked without a hello or a thank-you, as she thrust the letter at Louise. "I know my mother is saying something important. Is she saying what I think?" The beef, bacon, and onion of Ericka's flatladen simmered on the stove, its fragrance wafting into the living room, creating a sense of home that Ericka needed.

Louise flicked off her shoes, curled her legs under her, and stuffed a toss pillow behind her aching back. "Ah, Ricki, who am I to know what your mother means? She's a mystery to you and you've known her for fifty years."

"I just want your opinion. You see things I don't."

"Okay, I'll read it, but you may have to translate some words for me." By the time she finished reading, Louise's smile had disappeared. She paused, searching for the right words, weighing and measuring the situation as she always did. "I think she's sick, Ricki, or maybe even dying. That's what she's hinting. She wants you to come, to have a reunion or a final accounting before it's too late.

See that last paragraph when she admits she did wrong when you needed her and talks about time flying. Now she is imploring you to hear her message, to come to her, without directly saying so, probably because of her neglect when Ev was killed. How unfortunate in the timing of her letter, September 12, the day after the anniversary of his death when your pain has resurfaced. Still, her sentiment seems genuine."

"Just what I thought. So now, enough of her letter, and on to more important things—dinner—before the flat-laden dries out—and water for the sunflowers before they wilt." Ericka headed off to the kitchen with an urgency not matched by the state of dinner, for there was still plenty of liquid in the pan, the meat having at least another ten minutes to simmer before reaching optimum tenderness. Her mother was not entitled to another minute of her time. Ericka bustled around the kitchen, pulling out a trivet for the hot pan, straining the noodles and transferring them to a glass bowl, attacking the salad with great energy, and finally, placing the sunflowers in a vase in the center of the dining room table so that their brightness filled the room and said Louise was here. All the while, Louise sat and watched, not saying a word.

When the reasons for bustling evaporated and the silence had exhausted itself, Ericka pulled her chair up to the table, across from Louise, and announced, "So now we eat!" She scooped a huge serving of the meat on Louise's plate and decorated it with the liquid, the most delicious part of the dish, then sat a little straighter as Louise relished the taste of Ericka's creation. "It's good, I can tell by your face."

"Always good!"

Between bites of a well-cooked meal, they chattered about the school where they both worked—Ericka as financial secretary, Louise as registrar—and updates on the activities of Louise's girls, who were spending their usual Thursday night at their father's home. Finally, the crumb cake and coffee signaled the end of Ericka's culinary display. No more had been mentioned of the letter from her mother. The joy of the sunflowers had been dimmed by the growing darkness, their golden petals drifting inward. The dishes, empty of the home-cooked delicacies, had been scraped and nestled in the dishwasher. It was then that Louise, who had been waiting for the right moment, asked what Ericka knew she would ask: "So will you go see her?"

UNINVITED, EV SNEAKED INTO HER BEDROOM AS ERICKA turned down the comforter and fluffed her pillows. He usually stayed where he belonged after the burning ritual, but tonight, because of her mother's letter, he had reemerged. "When will you forgive me?" he asked.

She felt him standing behind her, his uniform on, his arms crossed in front of him, as if he were the one aggrieved. She knew what his face looked like without turning—his end-of-the-day stubble, his dark brown eyes that had once mesmerized her, his curly hair winning the battle against the pomade. Why was he bothering her? Hadn't he done enough when he was alive?

"Go away," she answered. "I will never forgive you." Three times he had betrayed her—first, by having an affair with his assistant; second, by telling her about it to assuage his guilt; third, by dying before he could properly atone, leaving her a loveless widow with a hollow grief. She had nothing to give Bella when Ev was killed—no joyful memories, no stories of a beloved husband and father, not even photos, all pictures of him alone having been destroyed the day he told her and the scissors having excised his image in any picture of the three of them.

Ericka slipped under the puffy comforter, pulling the billowing fabric over her head to blot out the unwelcome visitor, but somehow he had slid under the comforter next to her and was whispering in her ear. "My German sweetheart, you will always be the treasure of my life," he said, like he had whispered that first night in the hotel in Berlin, so filled with what her mother in the letter called *self-entitled optimism,* such a relief from the survival mentality of life with Mutter. She fought against the memory of his lips, his hands, the way they had made her—a sturdy, competent girl—feel soft and desirable. "Out of my bed," she told him, "Not yours. Mine. I paid for this house. I bought this mattress and this comforter with my hard-earned money. Not your bed. Out, now!"

But tonight he was being audacious, sensing her vulnerability, something all those years ago only he had bothered to see beneath her self-sufficient exterior, a vulnerability he had betrayed—there was that word again—when he had an affair and then told her. If he had kept his mouth shut, she could have blamed her imagination for wondering about his sudden rash of late hours and out-of-town trips. But no, not Ev. He had sat her down and with tears in his eyes apologized for what he had done and begged her forgiveness, as if his tears erased his culpability, his cruelty. Sitting there across from him, she had felt bulky, unlovable, the refuse of his life. She had wanted to kill him. And then ten days later, the terrorists did it for her.

"Go! Now! Or I'll get my butcher knife and slice you into flatladen!" But Ev refused to leave, lying quietly on what would have been his side of the bed if he hadn't strayed and if crazy terrorists hadn't turned the plane into the Pentagon. She heard his deep breathing, the way he sucked in all the air and then released it with a whistle as he drifted into sleep, the sound that reminded her she wasn't alone, that someone had chosen her, and she had chosen that same someone. She tossed off the comforter, Ev's body providing enough heat to warm her on a September night. He flipped his body, turning in her direction, his right arm suddenly splayed across her body, as if he owned her. "I don't want you," she insisted, then slipped out of bed and padded down the stairs, her left hip reminding her she wasn't the young woman he'd fallen for that night in Berlin. In the dark kitchen, lit only by the night light, she found her butcher knife just where it should be in the knife rack, cleaned and dried after her dinner with Louise. It was sharp, that she knew, having just sharpened it yesterday in preparation for the dinner, sharp enough to pierce Ev's body with one thrust. What had stopped her that night seventeen years ago? Not the tears in his eyes. Not Ev's comforting sweetness that complemented his firm body even after a sweaty ride home on the Metro. No, that sweetness had only made her want to kill him more.

All these years later, she remembered what had stopped her as he lay sleeping on the sofa. It was Bella, sleeping down the hall, who would be both motherless and fatherless if Ericka thrust the knife into his body. Bella had stopped her. But nothing was stopping her now. The girl was gone, the two of them unable to see eye-to-eye, both better off without the other. If only Bella had known what generosity, what love, what restraint Ericka had shown on that night.

She padded back up the stairs, one hand clutching the railing for balance, the other hand brandishing the butcher knife. No need for the hall light. It would awaken him and destroy her surprise attack. Besides, she knew the way by touch—when she had reached the landing midway up the stairs, when she had stepped onto the upstairs hall, when she should push open her bedroom door, how many steps to his side of the bed. She switched the knife to her right hand and raised it high above her shoulder to give more force to her thrusting movement, when suddenly the knife slipped from her hand, fleeing her cocked arm, dropping to the floor. And she saw what she should have seen—even in the blackness. There was no one in the bed, no disturbance of the comforter on the side where Ev should have been, no breaths to snuff out. He was dead, had been dead for seventeen years.

She shook as she stared at the knife beneath her feet, its blade reflected in the solitary beam of the street light. She hadn't realized the extent of her residual anger, as powerful today as then. Somehow the burning of the letter, the embers dying in the kitchen sink, the three hundred sixty-five days of solace until once again the calendar spit out the date of 9-11, the absence of physical evidence of his existence in the house he had never lived in—all had convinced her that she had exorcised Ev from her life. She collapsed on the floor, her legs no longer able to support her.

Waves of trembling claimed her body. She willed them to stop, but her body didn't follow her directions. At times her back stiffened with shooting pain. Sometimes her jaw clenched as if a fork lift would be needed to open it. And when the shaking had finished with her external muscles, it turned on her intestines, forcing her to crawl to the bathroom and purge everything she had consumed a few hours earlier. Finally, drained, she lay on the bathroom floor, praying for the energy to return to her bed, knowing that she deserved this pain for trying to remove Ev from her life and for failing so miserably.

If only Mutter's letter hadn't arrived the day after the anniversary of Ev's death, maybe he would have stayed buried. Once again, her mother had upended her life, this time with a letter that pretended to apologize, but was really manipulating her. Mutter never left anything to the whims of fate. She had deliberately timed that letter to arrive around the anniversary date, when Ericka would be most defenseless. She had wanted to reopen old wounds, so that Ericka—widowed, abandoned by her daughter—would in her loneliness be most receptive to her mother's fake love. But Mutter had miscalculated. Ericka's pain only reinforced why the woman who had rationed love, deserved nothing in return. Then fatigue took over, and she sank into a sleep so deep that Ev and her mother couldn't intrude.

SHE AWOKE TO THE FAMILIAR CHIME OF HER CELL PHONE on her nightstand. Her face, flattened against the tile floor, bore the temporary scars of the grout. She stood for the first time in hours, surprised that her legs had resumed normal functioning, surprised too that the sunlight was streaming through the curtains at such an early hour.

"Ricki, where are you? We are due in a front office staff meeting with the principal in four minutes. You're never late! What's wrong?" It was Louise on the phone, her voice frantic.

"Gott im himmel, what time is it?" She stared at the timer on the radio, which amidst all her Ev confrontations, she had neglected to set. "Almost ten. How can that be? Oh, Louise, never, never am I late! And now I oversleep. Please, tell the principal that I am ill, but I will be in by noon. She'll be furious. The reports she wants are on my desk. Thank you, thank you, my friend, for this call."

"Ricki, calm down. She'll understand. I was just worried after the letter and its unfortunate timing. I don't know what I thought."

"Trust me, Louise. Now it's all under control. No worrying, please."

But she was lying to Louise. Nothing was under control. Even her own body had turned against her. In the kitchen Mutter's letter, tossed aside on the counter, taunted her. "You silly girl, you think you can shut me out," the letter said, her mother's voice laughing beneath its silken German sibilants. Over four thousand miles and twenty-three years separated Ericka from the orderly flat she had shared with Mutter, an order that had traveled with Ericka to this home where it still taunted her. The pots and pans from dinner, scrubbed and polished and precisely aligned as if nothing had been cooked. The sofa pillows fluffed and returned to their assigned places as if Louise had never been here. Bella's forgotten clothes folded crisply in her dresser, as if Bella had never left.

Ericka wadded up her mother's letter and tossed it in the garbage where it belonged, but from the trash, her mother called out, "I'm still here. With Everett."

"So stay here, the both of you. I'm leaving!" And with that Ericka grabbed her keys and headed off to school.

USUALLY ERICKA OBEYED THE SPEED LIMIT, BUT TODAY her right leg could only press full throttle, all moderation of muscles having vanished. The roads at 11 a.m. were empty—no rush hour drivers, not even laggards—only a few isolated cars of seniors driving to their mid-day activities or stay-at-home moms with their toddlers buckled in the back seat. As she left her suburban development and headed north to school, they too disappeared. The country road belonged only to her, limitless, meandering, the crops in the fields mostly harvested but for the apples festooning the trees and the still-green pumpkins.

She lowered the windows, and the wind pummeled her face and tousled her neatly combed hair. But she didn't care because the speed reassured her that Mutter and Ev had been left behind in her house. Once she got to school, they would be gone, buried by the mind-numbing details of the staff meeting and later by the line of teachers requesting payments for this or that activity or depositing money for field trips and fundraisers. The sooner she got there, the faster the demise of the intruders. She watched with delight as the speedometer inched higher, sixty…seventy…almost eighty, reminding her of the autobahn and the exhilarating freedom it had given her. She gazed at the infinite sky that stretched over the flat fields and promised so much, not like her house with its unwanted visitors or the sky with the errant plane above the Pentagon. She loved it all—the intense sunlight, the puffy clouds, the azure canopy, the cawing crows, the steady symphony of the insects—all more vibrant and more perfect than her life, all fitting together naturally in a people-free universe that made sense.

"Ah, Mutter," she whispered to the sky that stretched from Maryland to Berlin, "if only we made sense. When I wanted your love and needed it most, you weren't there. Now you offer love, and I am closed off—not courageous enough to believe it's real, and if it is real, doubting its permanence. And so we go on, locked into September 12, 2001. Punishing each other and ourselves. And always, time flies."

In that moment of distracted reflection as her eyes focused upward, Ericka failed to see the sudden curve in the road until her car crossed the center line and invaded the opposite lane. She struggled to return the car to the right side of the road, but the momentum of the speeding vehicle resisted her belated attempt to stay within the lines that would lead her safely to school. When she failed, she slammed on the brakes, and her car spiraled across the empty asphalt, squealing and spinning despite her determined steering, finally bumping itself into a roadside ditch on the wrong side of the road, facing in the wrong direction. Dazed, attacked by airbags, a small gash bleeding on her forehead, Ericka watched a squirrel clamber onto the windshield and peer in at her bloody, startled face.

"Help me, Mutter," she cried out to the amazement of the curious squirrel and herself. The plea, she knew, applied not just to her battered car and body but to her whole life. She felt Mutter climb in beside her, cleanse the blood from her face, and say the words that began the letter: "Meine liebe tochter," words she both feared and craved.

Frozen

The predicted light snow was dusting the Dulles Toll Road and creating lace doilies on trees as drivers headed to Christmas dinners. But Ericka would have to settle for the limp tinsel on the international check-in counter and for whatever United Airlines served on the 6:59 p.m. departure to Germany. She was off to see her mother, her first visit home to Berlin in nineteen years, and certain to be her last if her mother's doctor was to be believed. Not the kind of Christmas designed to lift one's spirits.

"I hope the flight leaves on time," the heavy-set man ahead of her said to no one in particular, his gruff voice giving insistence to his words. "I've already missed Christmas dinner. I want to at least get to Berlin for leftovers."

Ericka wondered why the man was erasing with his grumpiness what little cheer the decorations provided. Still bundled in his overcoat and red plaid scarf, he seemed ready to return outdoors and restart the whole day because standing in this line on December 25 had never been part of his plan. She, too, had not planned to fly on Christmas day, but her belated decision to use her school system vacation to visit her ailing mother had left Ericka no other ticket option at a semi-reasonable fare. The bundled man harrumphed and shuffled his feet.

"This airport's like an oven," he announced.

"Save your fussing for something you can't control," Ericka responded, raising her voice to equal his. "You could unbutton your coat. That might help." She had already unzipped her parka and tucked her own scarf neatly in her carry-on. A little common sense could take you a long way in life, she thought.

The man scowled at her, then removed his coat and slung it over his arm.

"Better, isn't it?" she said, but no response followed.

Behind Ericka, a girl of about seven or eight whined as she clung to her mother, a pale woman with fuchsia streaks in her blonde hair. "I don't want to go. I miss Nanna and Papa."

"You'll see your Oma and Opa. They've been waiting for years to play with you. I'm sure you've got gifts under their tree."

"But they're not my real grandparents. It won't be any fun."

Fractured families, Ericka thought. The child had it absolutely right—they're no fun. But Gott im Himmel, did she have to whine so loud about it? Ericka imagined her eight-hour flight trapped in a middle seat next to this disagreeable child, trying desperately to get some sleep before her reunion with her estranged mother. With any luck, the girl and her mother would be seated in the back row next to the restrooms, far away from Ericka.

A desk attendant wearing reindeer antlers checked Ericka's passport and loaded her luggage onto the conveyor belt. As Ericka followed the human migration to the escalator to TSA, through the window she glimpsed a food transport truck with its windshield wipers going full-speed and snow accumulating on the tarmac. Maybe the rude man was right and the weather forecasters wrong—the flight could be delayed if the snow kept up like this.

Thirty minutes later she emerged from the subterranean inter-terminal train and trudged past newsstands and mostly shuttered food kiosks to Departure Gate 66. Outside the gate window, snow blew sideways and twisted into white tornadoes, making it impossible to distinguish the waiting plane from the sky or the ground. The clock read 5:05, one hour and fifty-four minutes until departure. The heavy snow line had obviously shifted south of Pennsylvania, where the Channel 4 weatherman had incorrectly predicted it would remain. People were already lined up at the counter, peppering the attendant with requests for flight changes or questions about connections. The heavy-set man plopped into the seat across from her, his coat selfishly claiming the neighboring seat as he called someone, maybe United, maybe his family, about the likely delay.

No sense getting roiled up before necessary, Ericka told herself. The plane was here. The crew was here. The snow could retreat northward and stop shortly. Just a de-icing and off they'd go—a little late. The fuchsia woman and her daughter had claimed the seats next to Ericka, the few remaining places near the boarding sign, as if proximity to the gate could stop the snow and accelerate their travel. "I'm hungry," the girl announced in a grating sing-song. "I'm hungry. I'm hungry."

"Could you watch our coats while I get her a snack?" the mother asked Ericka, her fruity cologne signaling youthful naiveté.

"Be glad to watch your things while you and the girl get some food," Ericka replied, relieved that the child would take her song elsewhere.

All the bustling about by the impatient travelers made Ericka almost excited about the trip, a long-postponed chance to say farewell at the urging of her friend Louise. She would kiss her mother gently on her cheek, squeeze her arthritic hand, and say the words she knew Mutter was waiting to hear, "I forgive you." Then Mutter would hopefully mouth the words "I love you" and put to rest all she hadn't been to Ericka for fifty years.

THE NOTIFICATION FLASHING ABOVE THE ATTENDANTS' desk elicited a rolling groan from travelers, including Ericka. *Delayed.* She had timed the trip stage by stage and brought enough reading materials to keep occupied for approximately nine or ten hours and a few snacks to tide herself over until dinner was served on the flight. It was now 6 p.m. Even if the snow stopped soon, with runway clearing and de-icing, dinner might not be until midnight, and a dinner that late would upset her digestive system, long acclimated to eating by eight at the latest. Ericka looked jealously at the little girl's half-consumed soft pretzel, then burrowed beneath her scarf and earphones in her carry-on to extract the home-baked sugar cookies and cranberry bread that Louise had insisted she take from her Christmas Eve gathering. As Ericka bit into the moist bread loaded with plump cranberries, she wondered if she should call Louise and let her know about the delay, but that seemed presumptuous when Louise would be occupied with her daughters at her parents' home. What difference did it make to Louise when she departed or arrived? What difference did it make to anyone?

The heavy-set man was yelling in German on his cell phone, loud enough for Ericka to make out the words. "What do you mean no one can meet me at the airport a few hours later? I travel all this way to see my daughter and she makes me take public transport. Again, it's my fault?" Ungrateful daughter, Ericka thought. You raise a child and sacrifice and then this thanklessness. Unless, Heaven forbid, the heavy-set man had been like Mutter, stingy with love, generous with criticism. Ah, it was none of her business— this loud man and his family logistics.

Once again Ericka dug into her carry-on, this time removing her earphones, not connecting them to her cell phone, instead using them to create a cocoon of silence. She watched the little girl next to her stretch her arms and pirouette in senseless circles, twirling faster and faster until off balance, she jostled Ericka and knocked her opened packet of half-consumed sweets to the ground. "Careless girl," Ericka said. "You've ruined my cookies and bread." The mother stiffened, pointed to the floor, and mouthed the words, "Say you're sorry." The girl, face scrunched like a prune, reluctantly picked up the smashed sweets from the grimy floor, wrapped them in the foil, and offered the reconstituted packet to Ericka.

"Too late. No good. Dirty." Ericka plucked the bread crumbs from her sweater and licked her fingers to salvage some satisfaction from what little remained of her treat. Then she pulled out her novel, angled her body away from the girl, and buried herself in the book. How good to read in German, she thought, the predictable rise and fall of the language, the orderly construction of the sentences, the familiar sounds and rhythm of her life before her marriage and its unfortunate demise. She would make the best of the delay despite the ill-mannered people nearby. She would forget about the wasted sweets, her growling stomach, and her dying mother. Soon, the snow would stop, the passengers would board, and she would get this farewell over with.

"ATTENTION UNITED FLIGHT 3342. YOUR FLIGHT HAS been canceled due to extreme weather conditions that show no signs of improving. Due to treacherous road conditions, local police advise travelers to stay in the airport until morning." The moans of the waiting travelers drowned out whatever else the well-meaning attendant was trying to say as a line instantaneously formed, snaking from the desk around the waiting area to the closed pretzel kiosk.

From her place midway in the line, Ericka called reservations to leapfrog ahead, but her call was met by an angry busy signal. The clock read 8:45, the middle of the night in Berlin where Mutter would be tossing and turning as she awaited Ericka's return in the morning, unaware that the visit was being upended four thousand miles away. "I've got no more than a few months," Mutter had explained when Ericka finally called in October in response to Mutter's letter, the first communication in a decade. "Soon there will be no time for talking." When Ericka had needed Mutter, when her own life had fallen apart—her marriage in shambles, then her husband gone—Mutter hadn't been there. Now Mutter needed her. In an unspoken rebuke, Ericka had procrastinated, finding work-related excuses not to travel, until finally with winter break upon her, there had been no more convenient excuses.

"Do it for yourself," Louise had counseled. "Not for your mother. Give your pain an ending, maybe even find release."

In retrospect, what it had taken to get here amazed Ericka. Re-reading her mother's letter until she could listen to Mutter's voice on the phone without dissolving. Re-living the memories of her childhood and Mutter's continued indifference until she had inoculated herself from the worst pain. Practicing the story of Mutter's absence when Ericka was widowed with a young child until Ericka could tell it to Louise without her voice cracking. Taking Louise's advice and committing herself to travel to Berlin, then informing Mutter of her commitment. Packing her clothes in the suitcase, tossing them out, and beginning again until the restless clothes stayed put. Finally, stepping into the taxi at her Maryland home and stepping out at Dulles Airport to start the physical journey. Now, from nowhere, attendants appeared and distributed thin, plastic-wrapped blankets, a sign that Mother Nature would be holding Ericka hostage at Dulles Airport.

STUFFED INSIDE HER THIN BLANKET LIKE A BRATWURST, head resting on her parka, Ericka had been trying to sleep for more than six hours. It was 5 a.m., but she couldn't ignore the snore-whistle of the heavy-set man and the perpetual body-shifting of the girl in the next seat, who periodically cried out in her dreams. Above, the heater hummed, pumping warm air into their refuge from the blizzard. Mutter—in her cotton housedress, hair pulled in a stingy bun at the nape of her neck—had made an appearance to chastise Ericka for her ill-fated travel plans and to repeat her grievances as she had done multiple times since the letter arrived. "Be still," Ericka whispered, so as not to call attention to her annoying ghost. "I've got already a new ticket for today—if the snow stops."

The lights stuttered, tentatively returned to full strength, then dimmed, eliciting a gasp from the insomniac travelers. "What the F--?" shouted a young man across the room. But there was no one at Gate 66 to answer his profane question, the staff having long ago retired to a secret room to rest before what was sure to be a stressful December 26. The absence of the perpetual hum suggested that the electrical malfunction had also affected the heat. Within half-an-hour, the frigid outdoor temperatures would likely seep into the defenseless terminal, and there would be no coffee or tea to stave off the cold, the remaining food kiosks having long ago closed. Nor would the workers, even if summoned from their sleeping areas, be able to prepare hot beverages if the main electrical system was on the fritz. From experience at her high school, Ericka knew that most backup electrical systems lacked the full power of the regular system and had a programmed priority of functions, likely keeping the thermostat at a survival temperature. She slipped into her parka proactively, wrapped her blanket around her legs, and pulled up the hood for warmth, cushioning, and sound-proofing. But half an hour later, sleep still eluded her.

Outside she could identify the shape of a giant flying whale parked in the gate and could differentiate clearly between ground and sky, both signs that the snow was tapering off. Soon, when she had a better idea when flights would resume, she would call Mutter and let her know the adjusted plans. But without electricity, she doubted the luggage carousels, the inter-terminal trains, the ticketing system would work.

The vulnerability of their shelter against the elements reminded her of Mutter's flat in East Berlin when Ericka was a child, after her father had died. Winter had made their lives even harsher—the food harder to come by, the coal rationed so that the landlord provided no heat at night, the frigid temperatures defining every aspect of their lives. But when the snow blanketed the dingy buildings and potholes and scraggly trees, she would gaze out her window and imagine a place as beautiful as the prince's castle in "Aschenputtel" and the possibilities of a better life. For years, like the German Cinderella, she had been treated as an unwanted stepchild by her own mother. A sturdy girl with a dour expression, she had hidden a spark waiting to be fanned. Then Ericka, too, had found her Prince Charming, who brought her to America and gave her an apartment that seemed like a castle and a beautiful child, and for one fairy tale moment, she had been loved. Now the husband was dead, the daughter estranged.

Her memories drew Ericka to the window where she pressed her nose against the glass and peered at the snow floating and twirling. She saw her young self spinning in the whiteness like the girl who had destroyed her sweets. "I'm coming, Mutter," she whispered. As the snow had covered all that was ugly in East Berlin, so their reunion would blot out the bad memories and allow her to once again love and be loved. On the horizon, a feeble shard of early light illuminated the snow.

SOMETHING WAS BUZZING AND VIBRATING. HER ALARM, time for school, Ericka thought, then realized she must have finally dozed off, that she was still trapped in the frigid airport in an uncomfortable seat with captive strangers.

"Your phone," demanded the heavy snorer. "Get the damn phone so the rest of us can sleep."

Sleep? Look who was talking, she thought. Ericka reached into her purse and saw a German number—not Mutter's.

"Ericka, this is Frau Schneiderman, your mother's neighbor. We've been waiting for you. Are you in customs still?"

"Frau Schneiderman, my apologies. There is a blizzard here, and my flight was canceled. I was waiting to call when I knew for sure when my rescheduled flight would take off. My apologies again."

"No, no apologies, Ericka. She is gone. Gertrud, your mother, she is gone. A few hours ago I came to check on her, bring her some tea, and it was all over. The doctor and the mortuary men are here, waiting for you. What should I tell them?"

The phone call left her speechless, causing Frau Schneiderman to shout in German, "Are you listening, Ericka? Do you hear me? Gertrud, she is dead," then repeat the news in English as if Ericka had forgotten her native tongue. It wasn't her hearing or Frau Schneiderman's linguistic choice that was making Ericka mute. It was everything else—the finality of death, who else to tell, whether to go to Berlin with no reconciliation and now no chance of one, and of course, what to do with Mutter. Not her body, those plans long ago made by Mutter, but with the essence of her mother—what she had and hadn't been to Ericka.

"Do what you must with the body. I know she has plans with the mortuary."

"And you, when will you be here?"

"I will call you soon, Frau Schneiderman, when I know. Danke schoen for all you are doing."

What was the sense of going to an empty flat? Why stare at a lifeless body? Why stand in the cold to watch the coffin lowered into the ground and pretend she cared? Get the refund on the fare, use the money for a summer vacation, she told herself. Go back to your warm home and call Louise. Ericka sat in stunned silence, unaware that the heavy-set man was staring at her or that the fuchsia woman had awakened and was looking at her with pity. She heard nothing. Not the man asking, "What can we do?" Or the woman saying, "We're so sorry." Or the attendant at the microphone announcing, "The electricians are working on the electrical system and hope to have it operational in an hour or two."

Food workers appeared with carts of stale pastries and bottled water. Sleeping travelers unfolded their bodies and ran their fingers through their matted hair. A baby wailed, and a mother slipped up her sweater to discreetly snuggle the baby to her breast. Under cloudless skies, plows hustled every which way on the tarmac, clearing away the foot of snow. But Ericka sat rigid, saying nothing.

The heavy-set man rose and crossed to Ericka. He took her cold hands in his glove-covered hands. "Let me help you. You have lost someone. What can I do? Who can I call?"

"No help is needed. None at all. I will turn in this ticket and go home as soon as I can get a cab. Frau Schneiderman will bury the body."

"You won't go to Germany?"

"Mutter is dead. Who would there be to see? Who would care?"

"She would care," he said, squeezing her hands. "You care."

"No, no, I don't care. Not one bit. It is over." There would be no return to the city that had defined her, no last look at the face that had haunted her, no absolution of Mutter's sin, no blessing of love upon Ericka. Near the exit, Mutter—in a nightgown and robe, her pinched face looking surprisingly like Ericka's own—was waving goodbye to Ericka and calling out, "See you later."

Lightning Bolt

Jamal imagined stroking the long, silky hair of Mrs. Friedenberg, his third teacher of the year. He had never before seen hair that beautiful up close. The rigid helmet hair of Miss Ericka, the woman he lived with for a short time, never appealed to his sense of touch. And Mrs. Rashid, the woman in charge of the house where he lived now, was too busy rushing around to be bothered with anyone touching anyone.

Mrs. Friedenberg's hair sometimes brushed against Jamal's face when he was invited to share her lunch and go over his letters with her. As she spread open the foil packages and put leftover noodle pudding filled with sweet raisins on a paper plate for him, she would lean close, and he wondered how it would feel to twirl her hair around his fingers. When the eating was done and she'd said a quiet prayer in strange words that made no sense to Jamal, she'd take his hands and squeeze them tight and say, "Now, Jamal, it's letter time." Her voice, as silky as her hair, anchored the letters that used to wiggle around on the page so that he couldn't tell a *b* from a *d*, and a *d* from a *p*. Sometimes she guided his finger over the shape of the letter, saying the sound over and over, then turning the sound into words, Jamal repeating the sounds until they became a song. "Puppy, papa, party, picnic," words filled with the joy of Mrs. Friedenberg.

When lunch was over and the other children had returned, Mrs. Friedenberg stood in front of the class and spread open her arms to welcome them back as if they had been away on a long trip, like his mother had been away since June. Sometimes he thought he saw a shadow fall across Mrs. Friedenberg's face, but then she'd flip her hair behind her shoulders and make a wide smile that sprinkled sunshine over the room. She loved them all, that Jamal could tell. But he knew he was her favorite.

One day in March, as the wind rattled the classroom windows, a girl with raggedy hair came into the class, holding the hand of the principal. "This is Kaneesha, and she is new here. We are so glad you have come to join us, Kaneesha," Mrs. Friedenberg said, using the exact words she had used when Jamal arrived in the fall, words that had belonged only to him. "Boys and girls, I know you will be kind and welcoming so that this classroom will become a wonderful place for Kaneesha just as it is for you." With that she rubbed Kaneesha's shoulders and guided her to an empty desk in the front row, right between Mrs. Friedenberg's desk and Jamal's. Jamal watched Kaneesha bow her head, as if looking at anything other than the desktop was painful. Then Mrs. Friedenberg leaned over, cupped Kaneesha's face in her hands, and whispered something to the girl.

When Mrs. Friedenberg turned to write Kaneesha's name on the board, Jamal leaned over and jabbed his finger in Kaneesha's side, then quickly withdrew his hand. Kaneesha winced, flicked her eyes in his direction, then bowed her head and studied the desktop again. Jamal noticed that Kanesha's pants were too short and her top strained at the seams—probably clothes that had been passed down by someone littler, like his cousin's clothes became his when he still lived with his mother. When Kaneesha finally smiled during Mrs. Friedenberg's crazy counting song, Jamal saw that she was missing lots of teeth and the ones left looked rotten. She would be no real competition for Mrs. Friedenberg's heart, that much Jamal had quickly figured out.

When Mrs. Friedenberg forgot to invite him for letter practice at lunch that day, he noticed that Kaneesha hung behind and took his seat next to Mrs. Friedenberg's desk, right in front of the picture of her husband with a wide-brimmed black hat, like a rapper, only he wasn't a rapper because Jamal had once asked and Mrs. Friedenberg had laughed and laughed. When Mrs. Friedenberg opened a foil packet and put it on a paper plate in front of Kaneesha, he wondered if it contained her delicious noodle pudding, or maybe her brisket that smelled of sweet cooked onions and didn't need much chewing even when it was cold.

"Is that your man?" he heard Kaneesha ask in a high-pitched whine.

"Yes, he is my very special husband."

"Where are your kids?" Kaneesha asked.

"You are my children," she answered, her voice skipping a beat like a rapper searching for the best words. "I haven't any children at home."

"Mrs. Friedenberg," Jamal called out from the doorway before Kaneesha's stupid questions could bring sadness to his teacher's eyes or make her hide in the supply closet. "I've forgotten my letters. My *p*'s and *b*'s are getting all mixed up." Then he started singing the song they'd made up—"Puppy, papa, party, picnic"—punching the air as he put an extra pop on each *p*.

"Oh, dear, Jamal. We'll have to practice them again tomorrow. Today I'm meeting with Kaneesha. Do you have your lunch card with you? Or do you want to borrow one?" He watched as she turned on her glow, and he could tell he was still her favorite. Of course, she had to meet with Kaneesha on her first day at school.

So he smiled back and said, "I'm okay with lunch. Hungry tummy!" and raced down the hall to the cafeteria as the principal called after him, "Walk, Jamal. Walk."

KANEESHA HAD BEEN IN JAMAL'S CLASS FOR TWO LONG weeks, but Mrs. Friedenberg was still holding her hand as she traced letters on the lined paper, and Jamal's invitations to lunch had become less frequent. When he was invited, he found Kaneesha already in the chair closest to his teacher and the picture of the black-hatted man.

That Friday, when Kaneesha stood in front of the class and collected their letter worksheets, Jamal swiped Kaneesha's from her desk and slid it to the floor. By the time she came to the last row, her row, he had already wadded up her worksheet and rolled it across the room. "My paper. I finished it, but it's gone," Kaneesha said to Mrs. Friedenberg. Jamal waited for Mrs. Friedenberg to say, "Well, I guess you'll have to stay in the principal's office during recess and do it again," but instead she said, "Don't worry, Kaneesha. I saw you working on it. We'll find it somewhere." Later when a chubby boy named Devon collected the number worksheets and Kaneesha's mysteriously flew into the trash can, Mrs. Friedenberg seemed genuinely confused. "What is happening to your papers, Kaneesha? Twice today they've vanished. Let's talk about this at lunch, after we come back from the library with books for the weekend."

Lunch? Jamal imagined Kaneesha sharing Mrs. Friedenberg's lunch alone, their two heads tucked close together. In the library filled with books that had been explored by many sticky fingers, Jamal plowed through the picture books, pretending he was searching for a special book when mostly he was thinking about Mrs. Friedenberg's hair brushing against Kaneesha's face and her liquidy voice repeating *p...p...p...* until the *p*'s became a shared melody. He tossed aside *Where the Wild Things Are* (too scary) and *The Little Engine That Could* (he'd heard this one far too many times) until he settled on a book with a cat in a red-striped hat and a bright red bowtie. He stood in line to check out the book, bouncing back and forth impatiently, until the librarian asked, "Do you need to use the restroom?" With these words, a plan was hatched. He'd go to the restroom, wait for the class to file down the hall to their own classroom, and then....

After giving the toilet a big flush so as not to make anyone suspicious, Jamal hid around the corner and listened for footsteps and Kaneesha's high-pitched whine. When she rounded the corner clutching her *Curious George* book to her fat belly, Jamal suddenly stuck out his foot, sending her sprawling across the linoleum floor, then disappeared in the commotion. Kaneesha sat crying on the dirty floor, cradling her right wrist, forgetting about her twisted book, which lay halfway down the hall, one page ripped at the top, another folded over.

"It's broke. Ow!" Kaneesha's wail echoed off the yellow cinderblock walls, and Mrs. Friedenberg dashed from the back of the line, her hair swaying back and forth. "Don't worry, Kaneesha. The nurse will know what to do." In seconds the principal appeared, followed immediately by a wheel chair and a nurse, who scooped the crying girl into the special chariot and pushed her down the hall past the first graders who watched the procession with a combination of awe and fear. That is, everyone except Jamal, who was doing his happy dance inside the boys' restroom and spraying water all around in celebration.

When Jamal returned to Mrs. Friedenberg's room for lunch, his shirt moist, his face sweaty, he expected to find an empty chair waiting for him, but instead he found Mrs. Friedenberg crying, her face gray as if covered by clouds. He had never seen her cry before, even though he once heard her blow her nose when she was hiding in the closet.

"I've forgotten my letters, Mrs. Friedenberg," he said. "My *b*'s and *p*'s are all mixed up."

She shook her head and waved her hand. "Not today, Jamal," she said, then buried her head on the desk.

"Don't cry, Mrs. Friedenberg." Jamal tentatively walked toward his teacher, who was making hiccup sobs that terrified him more than Kanesha's loud wail. "Please don't cry."

"Oh, Jamal, why did you stick out your foot and hurt Kaneesha? And you took her papers. Why?"

How had she figured it out? He was so fast with his hands and his feet, no one could have seen anything. Mrs. Rashid called him "Lightning Bolt," after Usain Bolt, who used to be the fastest runner in the world. Besides, how could Mrs. Friedenberg have seen anything when she was watching over all the other first-graders?

"Not me. I didn't do nothing."

"Jamal, please don't lie when Kaneesha's on her way to the emergency room. Some of your classmates saw you trip her. And a boy said you tossed a paper ball into the trash can. I've been very kind to you, Jamal. Can't you be kind to Kaneesha? Kindness is the most important thing to learn from me, more important than *b's* and *p's*."

"I didn't do nothing. Liars! They just hate me because you eat lunch with me."

"I've filled you with anger, not love. I've failed you, Jamal."

"I'll make you happy again. Let's have lunch. Or maybe I can come live with you and make you happy all the time." He reached out to her hair and started to twist his fingers through the most magical hair he had ever seen.

"No, Jamal." She reached for his hand that was entwined with her hair, but he bumped her hand away. "No, it's not right, Jamal. You shouldn't play with my hair. Not ever. I'm your teacher."

"But your hair is so soft." Even as she pulled away from him, he grabbed her hair, refusing to release it.

"Let go, Jamal." Mrs. Friedenberg clawed at his fingers to pry them loose, but he had wrapped the strands so tightly that no simple prying could free them. She clutched her hair frantically, as she shouted, "Stop, Jamal! Immediately! Stop!" The louder her voice became, the more vigorously Jamal pulled, using every ounce of strength to hold onto her hair, his eyes and nose and cheeks contorting into a desperate monster. The hair belonged to him, just like the chair next to Mrs. Friedenberg belonged to him, and their song and the noodle pudding and the sweet brisket—all of this belonged to him.

When she could endure the struggle no longer, Mrs. Friedenberg dug her hands deep beneath her hair and shouted, "There! You can have it, you naughty, selfish boy!" She flipped her hair upward until as one unit, it separated from her head and flopped helplessly like a dead cocker spaniel on Jamal's raised hand. She had removed her wig, prescribed by Orthodox Jewish rules to protect her modesty, and had exposed what should have remained hidden. Jamal stared at short, damp strands of hair pasted flat across a strange woman's head and at the hairy blob that lay lifeless in his lap. Now Jamal knew. The long, silken strands were not his teacher's hair. The ghost-like woman with red eyes was not the same woman whose smile sprinkled joy. And he, Jamal the Lightning Bolt, was not anyone's special child.

Bashert

"So my Rachela, if it's bashert, it will happen. If it isn't, there's nothing you can do." Bubbe was kneading the dough for the Sabbath challahs, pounding the dough especially hard with each declaration.

Rachel Friedenberg rolled her grandmother's dough into long strands and braided them one upon the other. "Not even praying to Hashem, Bubbe? Can't He make it happen?" Rachel asked. With each twist she remembered the changes in her own life since she had married Yossi. The excitement of her wedding night with the handsomest, smartest bridegroom in their Orthodox Jewish community. Cutting her gold-flecked brown hair and hiding it beneath a wig as required for modesty. The promise of fertility as she followed the monthly rhythm for sex and the purification of the ritual bath. The frustration as yet again she bled and no child took root in her womb. Now months of hope and sadness had become two years, the sadness sometimes following her into her classroom, the one place that had been her sanctuary.

"Yes, my Rachela, Hashem can bring miracles," Bubbe explained as she glazed the challahs with egg whites, "but He doesn't produce them on demand."

The chicken soup simmering on the stove should have comforted Rachel. But its fragrance only reminded Rachel that she and Yossi were still eating Sabbath dinner like children at her parents' cherrywood dining room table dominated by her mother's Sabbath candles and her father's wine cup.

"But Bubbe, how long till a miracle?" Rachel asked, then held back what she wanted to add. Her sister Chaya had married in the fall and was expecting, and her best friend Shoshannah already had two little boys that you couldn't keep quiet. But it was wrong to view life as some sort of competition and wrong to ask about the timing of miracles from Bubbe, who had been born in a displaced persons camp after the Holocaust.

Bubbe slid the challahs into the oven, set the timer, then held Rachel's face in her floured hands. "Dearest Rachela, Hashem makes miracles for His own good reasons, and we just put one foot in front of the other and go on with our lives, following His commandments. You are one of my miracles. Now go home and get ready for the Sabbath. We'll see you and Yossi at dinner."

Later that night Rachel and Yossi strolled home from dinner, their car off-limits for the Sabbath, his black fedora a muted statement of his total religious commitment. Other families, like ducks with their ducklings, hustled in lines down the sidewalks to put their little ones to bed. As the twinkling stars formed a canopy over Rachel and Yossi's path, she smiled at the children, tucked her arm in her husband's, and whispered, "It's like Hashem is making a special walkway just for us. He has plans." In the unexpectedly mild March night, he squeezed her hand, and his eyes sparkled. At home she removed her wig, perched it on its special stand, then came to him in his bed. He stroked her silken hair, then kissed the hollow in her neck. This is the night, she thought. Three weeks later, she bled.

Yossi suggested that she ask her doctor what they should do. "Will you come with me?" she asked.

"It's uncomfortable for a man to speak of such things. Besides, he might think less of me," Yossi told her as they washed the dishes after dinner in their galley kitchen that had just enough room for a high chair.

"Less of you?" Rachel asked. "What about less of me?"

Yossi blushed, then excused himself to work on a legal brief for an upcoming court case. It had become like this. Fifteen minutes together to eat, ten minutes of cleanup, then Yossi off to the spare room to work, and Rachel alone at the dining room table grading papers from her first graders, surrounded by bookcases overflowing with the wisdom of the Talmud and the law. By the time they were both in bed, the first one to hit the pillow was already asleep, or pretending to be asleep. Except on the Sabbath. Always then Yossi found time to do what needed to be done in the bedroom, the husband's duty.

Too shy to talk of such things with a doctor, Rachel instead consulted the rabbi's wife, an older woman so wise and generous that she was beloved by the women in the community. "So my darling, you are not yet with child," said the rabbi's wife as she brushed back a strand of hair from her wig. "There can be many reasons for this, some connected to Hashem, others of a more technical nature. So first things first. Tell me the names of your parents and Yossi's and where they came from." Rachel shivered from the stern gaze of the men and women in the framed pictures above the woman's chair, observant Jews who resembled her own family. Where are your children? their eyes said. What have you done to make up for the six million Jews lost in Europe? The rabbi's wife licked her pencil tip and scribbled on a yellow pad as Rachel recited the names and birthplaces that would constitute their child's lineage, a line stretching back hundreds of years to Poland and a renowned rabbi buried in the Cracow cemetery.

"Hashem needs a little help to extend this wonderful rabbinic line," the rabbi's wife announced. "There may be a little problem with how Yossi's seed flows. So put a towel beneath your hips to keep them tilted upward and the seed will flow where it needs to go to make a baby." Then she rolled a towel for Rachel, positioned her on the thinning carpet where her children and grandchildren had played, and taught Rachel what to do. "Have faith. Between Hashem and the towel, a baby will soon take over your apartment."

"And remember," the rabbi's wife added at the front door, "when Yossi penetrates, think only of Hashem's commandment to be fruitful and multiply—think of nothing else."

When Rachel explained the instructions to Yossi, he slumped at his desk. Later in their bedroom as he undressed by the dim street light, Rachel saw how thin he had become, the stress of their childlessness stealing his appetite along with his joy. Exactly as instructed, Yossi rolled the towel and placed it under Rachel's buttocks. "Am I doing it right?" he asked. "Yes," she said. When Yossi penetrated her, she willed herself to think of the fruitfulness of Hashem's world, not the rolled towel or the great rabbi in the Cracow cemetery. Instead, she thought of Kaneesha, the girl with the hand-me-down clothing, who every school day tucked her hand into Rachel's. And of Jamal, the golden boy with missing front teeth, who had wound her wig's hair around his fingers and demanded a mother's love she couldn't give him. She could feel Hashem's presence and the presence of children in their room.

Rachel didn't tell Yossi when the first pregnancy test showed a big "yes" because she wondered if he could tolerate a letdown if the test were wrong. She ran three more tests and then scheduled an appointment with the doctor to be absolutely sure. "Come home early," she begged him in a text after the appointment.

"Can't. Court tomorrow," he texted back. "Don't wait up."

At eleven she heard his car on the street, then his key in the front door. "You're up?" he said. She lifted her nightgown and drew his hands to her belly. He felt the smoothness of her skin and an almost imperceptible leavening, as if on this miraculous night, Hashem had descended to earth to plant a flower in the desert. He fell to his knees and pressed his lips to the belly of Rachel, who was bearing their child.

IN THE WEEKS THAT FOLLOWED, BEFORE THEY DARED tell their parents or Bubbe, they talked of whether they would move Yossi's desk to the dining room to make room for the baby in the spare room or if they would rent a house with space for many children, because naturally there would be others. They listed all the people they would tell—their families, his friends from Yeshiva and law school, her friends from day school and college, her relatives in Israel, his in California, and most important, the rabbi's wife, who had taught them how to position their bodies and what to think at the ultimate moment. They debated whether to send emails or make phone calls and decided that their joy couldn't be contained in a computer. When she grew fatigued or faintly nauseous, Yossi rubbed her belly, which somehow restored her energy and made the nausea disappear.

"I've never been so happy," he told her, his voice trembling on each word. "I was afraid…."

"Ssh," she replied. "It was bashert that we should wait more than two years for this great blessing. It makes our happiness that much stronger." Then she giggled uncontrollably, for the very idea of being a mother delighted her.

When she saw the bloody mess in the toilet, Yossi was out getting some milk. When he returned home, he found her weeping on the bathroom floor, traces of blood on the black and white tile. After the doctor scraped what was left from her uterus and suggested it was time to see a specialist, silence descended on their apartment. Yossi found infinite reasons to stay late at work—at least it felt that way to Rachel, who used his absence to cry without seeing his sunken eyes. Most of all, she didn't want him to see her doubt, not just about having a baby but about Hashem. She and Yossi both tried so hard to be good, but that goodness meant nothing to Hashem, at least when it came to their barren home. Maybe Hashem didn't exist, or if He did, maybe He lacked the omnipotence and compassion of Jewish teachings. Or maybe the shallowness of her faith, so readily upended by a childless marriage, had made Hashem turn on her. Maybe in fact, He was all powerful and all-knowing, and it was she who possessed the tragic flaw of not believing.

The specialist scraped and prodded and took their blood and their urine and specimens produced by Yossi in plastic cups. He examined them both inside and out on paper-covered examining tables and on digital images enlarged on a screen. Rachel's vocabulary expanded so that words like semen analysis and pelvic ultrasound replaced words like love and faith. The specialist's verdict would tell who owned their empty marriage—his semen or her eggs.

"It's fixable but there's no guarantee," the specialist announced, then proceeded to explain how a low sperm count, a low egg count, and a blocked fallopian tube were all inhibiting their fertility. First, relieved that she didn't bear full responsibility, then sad that Yossi had yet another burden in his life, Rachel began again to cry. "Fixable" meant thousands of dollars they didn't have, with law school debts and college loans still unpaid. And then what? Surgery on her fallopian tube, months of shots, lab dish mating of his sperm and her egg, implantation—and still, no promise of a baby, only technical manipulations designed to circumvent the emptiness that Hashem had set in motion.

"It's bashert," she whispered to Yossi as he wrapped his skinny arms around her in the medical building garage that reeked of gas fumes and bug spray. He, too, was weeping. "Better that we stop now than fall deeper in debt and suffer disappointment after disappointment. Better to say, Hashem has decided there will be no baby. We will go on with our lives. We will love our nieces and nephews and other children. We will find joy in the world, and we won't dwell on what we don't have."

"No child? To give up on a child? Maybe we can adopt." But they both knew that few Jewish babies were available for adoption, and it was premature to capitulate and dilute the lineage of the great rabbi of Cracow with an adopted baby not of Jewish heritage, who could never compensate for the rabbi's slaughtered descendants. Yossi drew out his handkerchief, sighed, and blew his nose. Rachel saw that with treatment, each night he would examine her body for signs of change. Were her breasts puffy? Was her belly expanding? Each morning he would leave for work, exhausted from dashed hopes. Each dinner he would try to eat what she prepared and try to talk about cheerful things, then retreat to his work so he could stop pretending. She might still have no child, Hashem would once again disappoint her, and she would have lost all that she loved most of Yossi.

"Better to have our mourning now," she said.

"Are you sure?" he asked. The grayness of his skin terrified her.

"I'm sure. It's bashert."

AFTER THEIR WEEK OF UNOFFICIAL MOURNING, YOSSI brought Rachel the biggest bouquet of roses on the Sabbath. During the week, he worked extra hard during the day, even forgoing lunch breaks, to be sure he came home at a reasonable hour. He praised her home-cooked cabbage balls and ate every bit on his plate, even when Rachel suspected that the food curdled his stomach. He made time on Sunday for an outing to the museum rather than to the park, which would be teeming with children. Yet when they turned off the lights and lay in their side-by-side beds, she watched sadness consume him.

"We need children in our lives. They can be ours, but in a different way," Rachel announced one day.

"Do you think we're ready for that yet?" Yossi asked. "Won't other children confuse us?"

"We'll test it and see," Rachel replied. "I've asked Shoshannah if we can watch Avi and Yakov on Sunday. Her husband's been feeling tired and needs a break from the noise, and she's with child again and overwhelmed. It'll be a relief for them and fun for us. You'll see."

"Of course," he said tentatively. "It'll be fun."

Avi and Yakov's arrival filled their empty rooms with tumult and laughter. Avi made funny spitting noises whenever Yossi tried to feed him and laughed when the applesauce sprayed on Yossi, which caught Yossi off guard and made Rachel giggle. Yakov pulled the cushions off the sofa and turned them into a tunnel, which he explored with Yossi as the engine and Rachel as the caboose. Despite the exhaustion of changing diapers and running nonstop to keep curious fingers out of electrical sockets, they agreed it was a good exhaustion. That is, until Shoshanna appeared and Avi and Yakov clutched her legs, and she smothered their sweaty hair with kisses, scooped up her boys, and left. In the quiet kitchen, Yossi stared at the blintzes Rachel had made as the cheese oozed out of the corners, like the applesauce oozing out of Avi's mouth. "Can we do it next Sunday?" he asked.

"Whatever makes you happy," she said as her jaw tightened.

"Does it make you happy?" he asked.

"Why wouldn't it?" she said, her voice wobbling.

By Thursday Yossi started planning the games they could play at the park when the boys returned. On his way home from work, he stopped to buy bubbles and a big wheel, and returned on Friday to buy blocks and Legos, just in case it rained. On the Sabbath, thinking about Avi and Yakov transformed his afternoon lovemaking. "That was beautiful," Rachel said. And Yossi beamed and repeated the lovemaking with even more gusto.

But on Sunday afternoon, when the boys left, silence again took over. While Rachel made dinner, he straight-

ened the apartment and tucked the toys away in the closet
and started imagining what they would do next Sunday.
When Yossi bought a miniature basketball hoop, the
closet could no longer contain the toys, so he stored the
overflow next to his bookcase. Soon the visits became
a ritual, as much a part of their lives as the prayer that
ended the Sabbath.

"What do you think about that Yakov? He's going to be
some basketball player—so strong, a great shot. And smart.
He already says the blessings and the pledge of allegiance. I
don't remember being that smart at age four." One Sunday
Yakov made a long-distance shot and Yossi shouted, "You're
the best!" Yakov shouted back, "I love you, Uncle Yossi."
That story became Yossi's favorite.

"What do you think about my boys?" he asked Rachel
at a Thursday night dinner, as he sopped up the last of the
stew sauce with a piece of challah.

"Your boys?" she asked as she wrapped the leftover stew
in foil. "They're Shoshannah and David's boys."

"You know what I mean. Of course, Shoshannah and
David are their parents, but they're our boys, too." Before
Rachel could refrigerate the leftovers, he stole a piece of
stew meat and popped it into his mouth.

"I don't think it's a good idea to call them our boys.
You can love them, Yossi, but there needs to be a line,
like between kosher and non-kosher." Her voice sounded
strained, other words lurking beneath. So Yossi kissed her
on her cheek and whispered, "Ssh, my Rachel. Let's not
fight. I'm so happy."

On Thursday as Rachel braced herself for the boys' Sunday visit, the thought of them taking over her home saddened her. She watched Yossi undress for bed, his belly now protruding as if he himself were with child. As he had grown plumper and more effervescent, she had become quieter and preoccupied with cleaning up after the boys, suddenly eager to have Yossi all to herself. How cruel to be filled with jealousy of two sweet little boys. She wanted to love the boys, but couldn't.

The only time Rachel felt truly alive was at school with the first graders, who were losing more teeth as the school year drew to an end and becoming increasingly energized. At home she counted the hours until the alarm would awaken her. At school she found reasons to stay late to clean out clutter for the summer or to work one-on-one with Kaneesha and Jamal before they left her classroom and her life forever—anything to delay her return to the apartment she and Yossi shared with Shoshannah and David's boys. She watched Yossi turn off his light and get under the covers, relieved that he hadn't approached her bed and stirred her feelings for him.

"I love you, Rachel," he said.

"I love you, too," she said mechanically, hoping that by restraining her love, she could become less jealous of the boys. As he lay with his eyes closed, she stared at the beautiful man who had once belonged only to her and longed for Sabbath afternoon, the only time she allowed herself to love him fully.

"Yossi," she whispered. "Why does Hashem give so unequally?"

"What?" he asked.

"Hashem gives so much to some, so little to others," she said. "Why?"

"What are you talking about?" he asked. "We have a wonderful apartment and good food on our table and jobs that give us purpose and friends and family." He paused and added, "And each other. We have each other, Rachel. How can we be selfish and expect more?"

Rachel swallowed what she wanted to say. "But she'll have three, and we have none." She tried to push away the image of a ripening Shoshanna holding two boys on her lap and Yossi hovering over the boys, but the image wouldn't disappear. Nor could she squeeze herself into the picture. Hashem was cruel, not like the Hashem she had learned about in school. How could she recite blessing after blessing in his honor when He turned away from her as He had turned his head when millions of Jews were slaughtered in Europe?

When Rachel awoke the next day, her bones aching, she forced herself to get out of bed. In the bathroom mirror her skin looked sallow, and her golden-flecked hair had lost its luster and started to fall out.

"My kindela," Bubbe said when Rachel visited that afternoon, "you're so pale. You are sick, dear Rachel?"

"No, not sick, Bubbe. Just working hard."

"Still, you are worrying about a baby? You have Yossi and Hashem. Dayenu—that should be enough."

Rachel took home her secret that no, she did not have Hashem, not in the way she should. They had abandoned each other. As for Yossi, she was losing him to Yakov and Avi. Tomorrow school break would start, and Shoshannah had invited her for lunch at the Bagel Shoppe, "my treat for all you have done for David and me." She would fix her wig with a special headband and color her cheeks with blusher and wear the new blouse her parents had given her for her birthday. She would try her best to be her old self, or at least enough of her old self, that Shoshannah wouldn't notice her sadness.

But she needn't have worried, for Shoshannah's boys were running up and down the narrow aisles between the tables with other little boys and knocking over Shoshannah's coffee when they bumped into her table. Shoshannah mopped up the spilled coffee and wiped leaky noses, not looking at Rachel, while nearby little girls in sundresses twirled like tops. When the excitement had subsided and the boys finally burrowed into their cream cheese bagels, Shoshannah took Rachel's hand and kissed it. "We'd be lost without you and Yossi," Shoshannah said. "You're the best friend in the whole world. All day the noise gets to me, and at night I can't sleep because the baby is kicking and then I have to go to the bathroom or one of the boys is crying because his tummy hurts or he has a bad dream. All week I say to myself, Shoshannah, if you can last until Sunday, then Rachel and Yossi will have the boys."

Shoshannah drew Rachel's hand to her belly and said, "It's kicking again. Can you feel the little feet? So much power for a baby. Like it's trying to compete with the boys for my attention."

Quickly Rachel withdrew her hand from her friend's undulating belly. Shoshannah had no right to complain when David only had to look at her and she was pregnant. Yakov and Avi climbed onto Shoshannah's diminishing lap, explored her face with their sticky hands, and rested their heads on her ample chest. "Off, boys. Enough already! Mommy's tired, and there's no room anymore for two boys on my lap."

What a selfish mother, Rachel thought. She who has so much should have much to give. Oh, Hashem, make our lives equal. Take away Shoshannah's round belly, and give it to me. I will love the kicking baby. I will be glad to be awake all night with the baby tumbling inside me. What's so bad about going to the bathroom? Look at what comes after—a little one with chubby hands and sweet kisses. As the yeasty smell of warm bagels sickened her, Rachel felt her stomach twist and turn for wishing such a horrible fate for her friend.

"I'm so sorry," she said. "So sorry. I've got to go." She pushed back her chair and headed for the restroom.

"Sorry? Go? What's wrong?" Rachel heard Shoshannah shout as she raced for the restroom and made it just in time. In the stall she heard Shoshannah enter and Yakov say, "Aunt Rachel, you sick?"

"Oh, Rachel, you're expecting," Shoshannah said as Rachel retched. "I'm so happy for you."

But there was no baby, only shame.

———————

WITH SCHOOL OUT, RACHEL HAD ALL DAY AND ALL NIGHT to think about her sinful wish. When Shoshannah's due date came and went, Rachel imagined the baby strangling on the umbilical cord, trying to escape but becoming more entangled. One night she thought she heard the baby crying for help, and Rachel begged Hashem to free the baby, but Hashem, if He existed at all, was being ornery, and the baby stayed trapped in Shoshannah. Rachel felt the baby slowly dying inside her friend and found it impossible to swallow. She gave herself the smallest portions of food, took a sliver on her fork, then consolidated the remaining food on her plate so Yossi would think she had eaten something. A few times she ran the water loud in the bathroom and stuck her finger down her throat to expel food that had slipped down into her belly. On Saturday she rebuffed Yossi's sexual overtures, saying she had a bad headache, knowing she didn't deserve such pleasure. On Sunday she fled the apartment before Shoshannah and the boys arrived, manufacturing an important errand for Bubbe, convinced that Shoshannah would read her guilty face.

On Monday, the seventh day past Shoshannah's due date, Rachel awoke and tried to get out of bed, but when she stood, her legs folded and she collapsed on the floor. She grabbed the nightstand and pulled herself up enough to fling herself onto her bed. That is where Yossi found her when he returned from work.

"Rachel, what's wrong?" he asked. He brushed his lips against her forehead to test for fever, then looked at her as if he were seeing her for the first time in months and recoiled.

"I can't walk," she said. She hid her face in her hands, but he peeled her hands away and shuddered at what she had become—sunken, colorless, hair thinning. Rachel wondered how her husband had missed the signs before. Amidst all his happiness, had Yossi chosen not to see how she had changed?

"You've been eating like a bird," Yossi said, trying too hard to be cheerful. "You need food. Let me heat you up some soup and toast a bagel."

"No food. I can't swallow." Who could swallow after willing Shoshannah's baby to migrate from her womb to Rachel's? Thou shalt not kill. Like a knife, her words had tried to rip the baby from her friend.

"You've got to eat." Yossi sounded desperate, as if he too would have blood on his hands.

"Not until Shoshannah has a healthy baby."

"What does eating have to do with Shoshannah's baby?"

Everything, she wanted to say. But instead she said, "I'm worried. The baby is overdue."

"So he's taking his time. No need to worry. It's you we need to worry about." He cradled her, saying "My Rachel, my Rachel, blessed be my Rachel," words he should have said long ago.

"Save your blessings for the baby. It's too late for me," she said.

"There are plenty of blessings to go around—for the baby, for you." Beneath the gentle words, she detected anguish, as if he saw himself reflected in her emaciated body. Too quickly he escaped to the kitchen, and she closed her eyes as the can opener whirred and the pots and plates rattled. When she opened her eyes, Yossi was entering their bedroom, carrying a tray, his face gray like in the parking lot after the specialist's verdict. "Eat," he ordered, lifting a spoon to her lips as she gritted her teeth to create a barrier to the invasion of the spoon.

She shook her head.

"This is about our baby, isn't it?" he said. "I've been thinking for a while that we ought to go back to the specialist, that it's too soon to say bashert, that Hashem would want us to keep trying. Somehow Hashem will provide the money."

"Hashem has already decided, if in fact He exists. I don't deserve a child."

"If He exists? Of course, He exists. And of course, you deserve a child. No one has a better heart than you. No one loves children more than you."

How clueless he is, Rachel thought. He can't even imagine the jealousy inside me. Or the destruction I've caused my best friend, or the evaporation of my faith.

"We are none of us perfect, Rachel. If we were, we would not be human." She knew he was talking about them both. Then he offered her a spoonful of soup, and she reluctantly swallowed.

Later Rachel lay alone in her bed. Beyond the closed door, she heard Yossi on the phone—his voice too soft to catch any words except her name. She knew now that there would be no baby because there could be no more marriage. In his face, the face she loved most in the world, she would always see her unspeakable sins and his months of indifference to her pain. And in her face, he would always see her ugly, twisted secrets.

The darkness consumed the dresser, the chair, the bed next to hers where Yossi had slept for two and a half years, their framed wedding contract on the wall. Rachel could not imagine anything redeeming ever happening to her again. Her hateful wishes had erased all ties to her loved ones and her community, and she felt a profound loneliness. Soon she, too, would vanish. She plunged into her hollowed-out soul and cried out in desperation, "Please, Hashem, if you exist, save me. Blessed be your name." Seven times she repeated her cry, each time more shrill, each time coming from a darker, deeper place inside her. Suddenly a burst of light, more intense than any she had seen before, radiated in the black room, its golden rays piercing Rachel's soul and illuminating her within. "Ah," she sighed with relief. "Hashem, you have found me." He existed. He could evoke miracles. She would survive.

Soap Opera Digest

When Stone brought Bella to live with him in the room he rented from his grandmother, Margie admired the young couple for all they had overcome—most importantly, Bella's mother's opposition to their relationship. The girl, a natural beauty with unruly hair, combined vulnerability and toughness, naïveté and resourcefulness. "She's just what Stone needs," Margie told herself. She cheerfully cleared the spare bedroom of stacks of old *Soap Opera Digest*, trash bags of bank statements and credit card bills, Rick's rusting fishing gear, and boxes of family pictures from her own parents—many of them featuring unidentified people who may or may not be relatives. In return, the young couple filled her bungalow with their odd-sounding music and laughter.

Margie couldn't keep her eyes off them. The way he rested his head in the girl's lap. The way the girl massaged his back after a tough day sodding lawns. The way Stone crooned to the girl when she was mad about something. Sometimes at night Margie would hear Stone and Bella in their bedroom at the end of the hall, the squeaking bed mixed in with other sounds she used to know. At first she felt embarrassed by the noises, then the embarrassment slipped away, replaced by memories from when she and Rick were first married and living in her parents' house.

It was like having *General Hospital* filming in her own home. Until Stone and Bella, Margie had felt closer to Sonny and Carly, and Luke and Laura than she did to her own family. Since 1988, she had followed their couplings and uncouplings on her favorite show, starting when she was a stay-at-home mother and later when she babysat her grandson Stone and of course, when she was housebound by her husband Rick's heart troubles. Despite the daily turbulence of her t.v. family, Margie found comforting predictability in their essence. Sonny—the mob boss with a heart of gold for his family. Carly—his tempestuous wife with a ferocious protectiveness of her children. Luke—the passionate anti-hero. And Laura—most of all, Laura—who had loved faithfully and purely, and who had endured so much with Luke until he retired from the show.

Sometimes late at night, under the watchful eyes of Rick's picture, Margie wrote the script for Bella and Stone in her mind. The girl would tame his wildness, and down the road, they would have children—a boy and a girl—the boy with his father's rambunctiousness, the girl with his mother's resourcefulness. In the beginning Margie played the wise older woman role and provided advice to Bella and Stone: "Just give him a chance. You can make a real man out of him." "She's a sweet girl. Show her that you love her." But lately as the noises from their room changed to shouts and frequent door-slamming, sticking with the script had become challenging.

One wet Tuesday, just as the local news switched over to Lester Holt, Bella returned from work, her face drawn, her CVS uniform dripping from her backpack. She plopped onto the living room sofa without even removing her sneakers and buried herself under the red and gold team afghan

Margie had crocheted for Rick. Everything about Bella called out for loving, but Margie had been barked at too often in the last week by the couple to ask how the girl's day had been. Instead, Margie simply nodded and went about her business making dinner for the three of them. Her grandson would have to deal with the girl's petulance when he got home. When she was like this, she was Stone's issue, not Margie's, unless you considered the overdue rent and board, two months overdue, but who was counting? Somehow missing rent payments had never become an issue for Luke and Laura when they hid away in Beechers Corner. But then Laura hadn't taken long showers morning and night.

"Where's Stone?" Bella demanded, her sullen face peering out from the afghan. "He promised to pick me up after work but never showed. I texted him, but nothing."

"Maybe they gave him overtime. Lots of people are getting their lawns spruced up for spring." She wanted to add, "Do you mind setting the table?" but thought better of the request, given the cloud suspended over Bella's head. Instead she asked, "Are you hungry? I'm making some spaghetti."

"He could've at least texted about the overtime. I had to change busses at the mall, and it was damp and cold standing out there. If I'd known he was going to bail on me, I would've asked Enrique for a ride. But he'd already left by the time I figured out Stone wasn't coming."

"Why don't you text him again or call him? See if he'll be late for dinner. I hope his cell battery isn't dead. The way he's on that thing night and day, the battery doesn't last long at all."

Bella flung the afghan to the floor, pulled her cell phone

from her jeans pocket, and stomped up the stairs. Margie could hear her voice the whole way in the kitchen—something about how dare he strand her again, she'd never do it to him, what good was he if she couldn't count on him. Margie almost felt sorry for the girl, even though she'd changed into more of a tempestuous Carly than a dependable Laura.

"He'll be home late. He says to just put his food in the refrigerator." Bella was standing in the doorway, her eyes puffy, her chin jutting out like a spurned wife. "Bastard." She grabbed a wad of napkins, yanked open the silverware drawer, and slammed dishes on the table for the two of them.

"Thanks, dear." The word "dear" felt strange in the context of the girl's battle with the kitchen, but Margie had never called Bella anything else.

"He's an ass, you know. To you and to me. Even if he didn't return my texts, he should've at least called you about being late for dinner."

Margie said nothing. What could she say about her own grandson, who'd been turning into an evil twin of his old self? In his defense, he'd been half-raised, if you could call it that, by an irresponsible mother. Still, Bella had a point. When Stone had no place to go after high school, she'd taken him in and then the girl came along. Stone owed her something for that.

Margie and Bella stared at each other across the food, their feet resting on the picture boxes now stored under the table. The steam rose from their pasta and the canned spaghetti sauce she'd doctored with onions, garlic, and the fat meatballs Rick used to devour even when the doctor said red meat was bad for his heart. Bella stabbed her fork into the spaghetti and slurped it loudly. Margie wished she'd say something. At the start, the girl had been full of chitchat—about music and people she and Stone had gone to high school with and the English course she was taking at Montgomery College—and Margie had felt her blood stir like it hadn't since Rick had been hauled away by an ambulance. The girl had even listened to Margie tell how she'd made something out of Rick, stories no one else pretended to listen to anymore.

When the empty plates signaled the end of dinner, Bella helped clear the table and wash the dishes. No words were spoken except what was logistically necessary, such as, "Do you want me to soak the sauce pot?" Then Bella disappeared into her room. Before long, the sweet smell that Margie had learned was marijuana wafted down the stairs. After Margie had made a fuss about refusing to be a party to a crime, to her surprise, no police had knocked on the door to arrest anyone for possessing an illegal substance. Recently, she'd come to appreciate the calming effect of the drug on door slamming.

Margie settled in with her *Soap Opera Digest*, curling up in the Barcalounger Rick stretched out on when his feet swelled and wept. According to one insider, it looked like Sonny might be leaving or at least going on a long hiatus. That would be too bad. Without Sonny, the show would lose the sexual tension between Sonny and Carly that made the story so exciting. Over the years, Carly had taught Margie that your husband could have a fling and many episodes later return to beg for your love, which, of course, you would give because his love was worth it. Until one day, death would finally rip him out of your life, and you would be left with memories of his crooked smile that tore your heart out. She quickly murmured a prayer that Sonny would survive his latest escapade.

She couldn't wait for Stone to come home. Maybe he'd sashay in and sing out to the girl upstairs, "Belle, my Belle, miss my Belle." He always called her Belle, a name that signaled she was his alone. What a voice Stone had—deep and simmering like his grandfather's. He hadn't been singing much lately. But if he did, if he sang just right, then maybe the girl would walk tentatively down the stairs and flip his hair back and stare into his eyes, then trace the shape of his lips with her finger, then wait—maybe even for a full minute—until Stone leaned in and kissed her, tender at first, then as she relaxed into the kiss, with strength and power.

Margie was watching *Dancing With the Stars*, and a C-level celebrity was doing an offbeat tango to a song that most definitely was not a tango, when Bella appeared in the living room with her duffle bag, a backpack, and the fluffy pillow that she'd brought from home when she first came.

"I'm leaving," she said. "I want to thank you for putting up with me, but Stone and me are over." She shifted her feet as if she had more to say.

"Well, dear, shouldn't you wait to talk it out with Stone, give the boy a chance to make it up to you? Isn't this a bit rash? I mean, where are you going? Have you and your mother made amends?" The words tumbled unedited from Margie's mouth. Bella stirred her—the girl's face washed out by sadness, her loose curls tumbling every which way, the pillow comforting her like a child's teddy bear. She wasn't a bad girl, Margie admitted, even when she was cussing and slamming doors. Where was Stone? He needed to be here.

"I'm spending the night with a friend, then I'll find someplace where they don't need a room deposit. Stone owes me about $300. Tell him that it's your money now, back rent from me." She looked sheepishly at Margie and clutched her pillow, as if she expected Margie to chastise her or seize her belongings as collateral for her debt.

Margie grabbed the arms of Rick's Barcalounger to prevent herself from springing to her feet and hugging the girl tight. She imagined herself saying, "Oh, dear, you don't owe me a thing. I'm just going to worry myself sick about you and where you're sleeping and how you'll get your next meal and where you'll get the bus fare to get to work and how you can concentrate on English class with all this craziness. Can't you stay to talk with Stone? Or at least, let me give you $100 to help get you started." But Stone wasn't home, and she didn't have $100 to spare, what with the water bill overdue. Besides, hugging like that always meant someone was leaving the show for good.

"Well, good luck, dear," Margie said, giving as much as she reasonably could. The girl turned and left without another word. She'll be back, Margie told herself. She's got to come back. True love always has its ebbs and flows.

Playoffs

I t took Stone only five minutes to persuade Bella to come with him for a beer at The Green Turtle. The way his grandmother had described Bella's calm determination when she left with her duffle bag and pillow, he thought that she'd passed the point of truly caring about him. Usually, when she claimed he'd done something wrong, her paranoid anger spilled out for at least an hour, followed by a great makeup session as one passion morphed into another. But tonight she'd come without a shouting match and without his begging, which confused him.

Bella maneuvered into his KIA, using the driver's side because of the banged-up door on the passenger side from an accident that wasn't really his fault but had provided a temporary insurance windfall last summer. As she wiggled across the console, he studied her peach-like ass, the first thing he'd noticed when he'd seen her at a party in jeans that stoked his imagination. "You go ahead and pick the music," he said. He could tolerate a few minutes of Beyoncé if it put Bella in the right frame of mind, even with all her bellowing about that woman stuff.

"Not in the mood," she replied, then turned her head to stare out the passenger window as if something important flickered in the silent darkness. No sense apologizing when he couldn't look her in the eyes and send unspoken love-texts, though he had to consciously resist reaching for her thigh.

The Green Turtle Sports Bar was packed for a Wednesday night, filled with boisterous red-shirted fans, not the regulars who felt more comfortable here than home alone. In all the excitement about forgetting to pick up Bella at work and her abrupt departure from their room at his grandmother Margie's, he'd given no thought to game six of the NHL Eastern Conference hockey finals. He felt strange wearing a band logo shirt amidst a sea of red, a betrayal of his Caps—his third-favorite DC sports team—who had never before in his twenty years made it this far in postseason. He'd have to tell Bella that, after they were settled in the booth. Forgetting about such a make-or-break game because of her would show how much she meant to him.

"So I'm not coming back. Just wanted to put that up front before we talk." Bella slid into the booth, taking the outside seat and throwing her hoodie next to her, which forced Stone to sit on the other side, his back to the t.v., and stare at her cold gray eyes.

He flashed the smile that had made her melt the first time they'd talked junior year, a smile he knew would make her take back her crazy declaration. "I know, Belle. You're angry. You've got every right to be." He dialed back his smile and let his eyes take over. "I just want to chill with you, leave us as old friends, not enemies. It's too many years to throw away." An ear-shattering cheer went off near the bar, and Stone had to resist turning to see who had scored and how, knowing that a glance over his shoulder would doom the night.

"It's over, Stone. I've got to get somewhere in my life, not stay stuck in Stone's world."

"Shit. It's that Enrique. That's what this is all about. I'll bet he gave you a ride home and you had someone new to listen to your sad stories about your mother. *My mother said I stole from her. My mother threw me out. My mother never saw who I am.*" Stone paused long enough to soak in the cheering in the bar that hadn't yet subsided, a long overdue release of playoff fever that stirred something in Stone almost like sex.

"Go ahead. If you think it's about Enrique, watch the replay," she said flatly. Taking that as permission, he turned briefly toward the big screen while Bella took her lip gloss from her pocket and applied it over her lips three times. When he turned back, his face flushed from the goal, the sight of her thick, shimmering lips evaporated his lie that all he wanted was friendship. Enrique or no Enrique, he stuck out his foot and rubbed his ankle up and down her leg, singing sweetly, "Belle, Belle, come back to me. No one else gonna love you girl, half as much as me." Even though her leg retracted at the touch of his ankle, Bella wasn't stopping his singing, which she'd always loved because it soothed all that junk tossing around inside her. As her face relaxed, he remembered he needed her in more ways than he could ever say aloud. More ways than just the sex. Even things that bugged the shit out of him, like her demands that he work, not just hang around his grandmother's house, he needed. It was good to get paid, good to have achieved something tangible during the day, even if lugging sod and digging holes in packed clay soil exhausted him. Bella made that happen for him, too.

The server, a tall skinny girl, with tiny breasts pressing against her Caps shirt, had suddenly appeared and brushed her hand across his back. "Hey, Stone. Haven't seen you for ages. Want your regular?"

He nodded as she tucked her red-streaked hair behind her ear and recorded the order on her tablet, her perfume reminding him of the one time he'd gone home with her.

"And you?" She looked toward Bella, belatedly noticing that there were two people at the table.

"Just a coke."

"Hey, Lulu," he called out to the server who had already moved on to the next table.

"Give me an extra-large side of onion rings. You da best, girl!" He was starved after a full day sodding and the slight buzz from the beers he'd shared with the guys, and Margie hadn't even kept leftovers for him, as if she'd been personally insulted by her grandson's forgetfulness toward Bella.

"No problem, Stone. Gotta keep a hungry man satisfied."

Bella was fiddling with her cell phone, bending over so far that all Stone could see was the scrunchie containing her fluffy hair, a requirement at her drugstore, which frowned upon stray hairs on cough medicine and toothpaste. He started singing again, this time in a deep, slow moan, to show her how much she really meant to him. But when she looked up from her cell, her lips had straightened into a line rebuking him for something he couldn't quite figure out.

"So this Enrique dude, you and he are a thing now?" He could imagine Enrique coming on strong in the car, putting his arms around Bella when she sobbed about Stone leaving her at work and poured out all the old stuff about her mother as if she'd never ever told anyone else in the whole world.

"This isn't about Enrique. I'm too busy at school and work to waste time crying over you and wondering if you will or won't be where you promised to be or losing sleep because you said something stupid. You just want to make it about Enrique, so you feel entitled to watch the Caps replay or flirt with the server."

"If it's not Enrique, I don't get it. Three years, Belle, you don't throw away three years of great sex. And no one else can get me out of a funk like you. "

"That's what I mean. Everything's about you."

Another loud roar reminded him that at least things were going well with the Caps, considerably better than things with Bella. "Belle, I'm sorry about forgetting to pick you up. I got paid and had to get my check cashed to pay back some guys. And then one thing led to another and my cell was dead."

"I've heard the story before. Over and over." She looked like she wanted to say more, then stopped and licked her lips, lingering an extra second on the top lip, pulling her tongue back into her mouth, rubbing her lips together, drawing him toward her as he remembered her fruity taste, her ripe sweetness after a day at the drugstore. He lurched onto her seat, forcing her body to slide onto her hoodie, crushing her into the other side of the booth, so tight into her that he shared her deepening breaths.

"Get away," she growled, pushing her hand against his chest, but not too hard because he could tell she was feeling his love.

"You want me. You know you want me," he whispered as grabbed her hand and pressed his lips onto her neck. As drunk with Bella as he'd ever been, he sucked her into him—her smartness, her practicality, her toughness mixed with vulnerability—everything she was that he wasn't.

She stopped pushing, letting him do what he wanted until Lulu said, "Hate to interrupt, but here's your drinks." The server stared at Bella's red cheeks and the purpling bruise on her neck where Stone had devoured her, then left without another word. He wanted to say how much he loved her, but instead, he chugged his beer until his stomach rebelled with a huge belch, then laughed when she lifted her eyes. When she didn't react, he reached up and removed her scrunchie, and her hair tumbled across her face, spirals of inscrutable curls, twisting one upon the other, his fingers exploring every curl as she drew deep on her straw until a loud gurgle insisted she'd hit bottom. He laughed again, pulling her toward him, yanking the straw from her amazing lips, pushing his against hers, feeling an unfamiliar passivity but pushing all the same.

"We're in a restaurant, not at home," she said when he came up for air. "Enough."

"What the hell, Belle! What do you want? I'll do anything you want. You da best, girl."

"I thought that title belongs to Lulu."

"But I mean it with you. There's no one I love like you. Give me another chance. What do I gotta do?"

"Hmmm. Let me think. Oh, I know. You can start by paying me back the $300 you owe me."

"I say love, you say money? Anyways, I don't owe you that much. I just borrowed money once or twice to make my car payment."

She fished in her pocket, pulled out a wrinkled piece of lined paper, and began to read. "October 1—$50 for car payment. November 5—$50 for credit card bill. December 22—$100 for Christmas gifts. February—$40 for gas. March—$60 for an emergency supply of weed. For a grand total of $300. And that's only the loans I bothered to write down."

"I know I paid you back for the early ones."

"Are you kidding? You've hardly ever repaid me for anything, not even for a Big Mac. And now I'm late on back rent to your grandmother, and I've got to get tuition together for my summer course and books, and I'm sitting on $300 of your unpaid loans. So, yes, that's where you can begin—by paying me back."

"I'd give it to you if I had it, but I don't."

"Liar. You just cashed your check today. Remember? That's why you forgot about me and my aching feet."

His wallet, swollen with money, pressed against his ass, less than the $300 she was demanding, but all that he had after forty hours of hard labor minus the money he'd given to the guys for beer. "Yeah, you're right. Technically, I've got money, but it's all owed for rent and my car payment." Not really true, but close enough that it wasn't an outright lie. Besides his sore muscles would be a total waste if he went back to Margie's with an empty wallet. Still, an empty wallet was better than an empty bed.

"Let me see what you've got."

"Belle, let a man have some pride."

"It's your choice. If you want a chance with me, I need to see the money."

He counted it out, stacking it neatly on the table, feeling each lift of the shovel as he recited, "Twenty, forty, sixty, eighty, …" and stopping finally with, "$263, the total of my money, and most of it isn't even mine." The loud groan behind him signaled an unfortunate turn in the Caps game, maybe even disaster as Bella walked her fingers toward the pile of money on the sticky table, until she covered the stack with her hand, then slid the stack back toward herself with an unexpected sadness.

"All of it?" he asked. "Not even thirty bucks for the burger, drinks, and tip? I can't stiff Lulu."

She plucked a twenty and a ten from the stash and folded the money into Stone's hand, her hand lingering atop his, signaling what? He had stopped reading her right tonight, that much he knew. He leaned over and kissed her, this time on the cheek, wondering what this half-assed kiss would cost him. She stuffed the money under her shirt, fumbling around to wedge the money into her bra.

"You think I'm going to steal it?"

She shrugged.

The burger had miraculously appeared, and he noticed that the kitchen had been stingy with the onion rings. He bit into the burger, letting the juice dribble down his chin. Bella reached for a napkin and dabbed his face, then dangled an onion ring above his mouth, pulling it away when he dove for it, before finally feeding it to him. Then another. And another, her laughter building as he consumed each offering.

"So you're coming back," he said. "I'm glad."

She grazed her hand across his cheek. "I can't," she said with a firmness that contradicted her touch.

Her push and pull, like the ebb and flow of the hockey game behind him, confused him, depressed him, excited him, angered him. She had his apologies and his love and his money. What more could she want? Besides, who the hell needed her when Lulu would go home with him in a minute? But the thought of the skinny, predictable substitute made him feel the emptiness without Bella.

"One more chance, babe. I paid you back without even a fight. You can see how much I've changed, and it's all because of you."

But she was waving to a guy at the door. Was that short guy Enrique from the drugstore? Who cared? If she was satisfied with that dork, let her go. Shit, the shrimp was smiling and walking toward Bella with a confidence that said he was expected. A deafening roar exploded around him, another goal for the Caps, leading them to more post-season triumph, maybe even to the Stanley Cup. Had he missed a pivotal power play? He'd waited for this his whole life. Stone grabbed his burger and headed to the bar to see whether it was Ovi or Backstrom or Oshie who had scored, trying hard not to think about Bella and the asshole who was sliding his arm around her waist, forcing himself to forget about tomorrow, filling himself with orgasmic expectations of game seven.

The Fixer

S tudents often waited in long lines to speak with registrar Louise Krauss. In the fall, stress etched on their faces, procrastinating seniors pleaded for her to rush their school records to meet college application deadlines. And at the end of the admission season, students left out in the cold by their favored colleges sought comfort from the registrar, her round face and sunny smile inviting them to open up. Her talent for repairing their lives traveled beyond the students to their parents, including to Mr. Daniel Lefcowitz, father of Abe Lefcowitz, the most brilliant member of the STEM Magnet at the highest ranked high school in all of Montgomery County. At least, that's what Mr. Lefcowitz asserted about his son when he charged into Louise's office and demanded to know what had happened and how she was going to fix it.

Normally the Guidance Office would be the first stop for frantic parents when their students were locked out of the most competitive colleges. But on this particular Monday, all the counselors were in an emergency meeting regarding their administration of the upcoming Advanced Placement exams and the loss of a nearby church as a testing site because an oak tree had smashed its roof during a wind event yesterday. So it was that Mr. Lefcowitz burst into Louise's tiny closet of an office, waving a fistful of rejection letters and reciting his son's resume: "4.0 unweighted GPA, 1520 on the SAT, countywide finalist for the National Science Talent Competition, state finalist for National History Day, county tennis champion for two consecutive years."

Louise spun her chair so that she could face Mr. Lefcowitz directly and nodded in rhythm to his recitation. She made sure that her eyes engaged his and that her expression suggested genuine concern. She watched Mr. Lefcowitz's face redden and the red soften to pink as he completed the recitation and sank into the armchair next to her desk, burying his face in his hands.

"Mrs. Krauss, I don't know what to do. A brilliant boy and no place to go to college. I knew Harvard was a longshot, and so were Yale and Princeton, but Tufts? For goodness sakes, Tufts and Penn and Colgate? At least one of them should have accepted Abe. What am I to do?"

If Louise had become callous after ten years as registrar, she would have heard only the *I* in his question and labeled him a helicopter parent. But she had lost sleep herself over her own daughters' ups and downs and the strains they still felt because of their parents' divorce, amicable though it was. Thus, when Louise thought of the involvement of Mr. Lefcowitz, the word that came to mind was *empathy*—a natural outgrowth of a parent's love. As he lifted his head and looked at her with misty eyes, Louise passed him a box of tissues, waited for him to blow his nose, then said, "It's horrible, Mr. Lefcowitz. But we can do something."

He sat up straight in his suit and crisp dress shirt. "We can? Of course, we can." Then he paused and added, "But what?"

"We'll work three paths and see which yields the best result. Is Abe waitlisted at any of his schools?"

Mr. Lefcowitz nodded. "Tufts, Penn, Colgate."

"Good. Then I'll begin by calling the admissions office of one of these schools and offering official testimony on his behalf. Abe will have to pick one because the school will want assurance that Abe will accept if they pluck him from the waitlist. Path two involves my calling other less competitive schools and seeing if they have vacancies. When they hear of Abe's sterling credentials, they may jump at the chance to capture such a great student. Path three entails Abe finding an interesting internship or travel opportunity for the first semester and calling the waitlist schools to request a second semester admission. Illness and personal issues often send students home mid-year, and some schools like to fill those vacancies. Now none of these is an ideal way to begin college, but we're past ideal at this point. So, go talk with Abe. Tell him to let me know by tomorrow morning what he'd like to do."

Mr. Lefcowitz flung his arms around her, squeezing her as if their relationship had deep roots. "Mrs. Krauss, you are an absolute angel. I thought it had all been for nothing— those sleepless nights, his weekends researching in the lab when other kids were playing, the nonstop sacrifices of my boy's life. And for what? Now you are making it happen." He leaned forward to squeeze her again until she pulled back, her pursed lips and flushed face reminding him that she was, after all, an MCPS employee.

"No promises, Mr. Lefcowitz, only untested possibilities. One way or another, this year or next, Abe will go to college and do just fine."

"That's all I wanted, Mrs. Krauss. Hope."

As the father turned and left, his aftershave lingered in the room—crisp, bursting with energy—like Mr. Lefcowitz himself.

TUESDAY LOUISE ARRIVED AT SCHOOL WITH A SLEEP-deprivation hangover following late-night fretting about her oldest daughter Samantha's low history grade and what Sammi saw as its potential impact on her GPA and as a result, on her entire future. The pile of updated-transcript requests on Louise's desk had exploded over the past week, and her email was clogged with urgent messages from the Head of Guidance about Louise's responsibilities as a result of the revised Advanced Placement testing plans. As her head throbbed, Louise could tell that most of the day would be devoted to drudgery.

It was a relief when mid-morning, the main office called her to pick up a delivery. She entered the office, expecting a box of forms from Advanced Placement, only to discover the main office staff encircling a huge spray of hydrangeas, calla lilies, and hot pink roses. "For you," the business manager, Ricki, announced. It wasn't her birthday, and her ex hadn't done anything that required a lavish apology. Besides, Mike had never thought in terms of floral tributes, not even on Valentine's Day when they were first married.

"Open the card," Ricki insisted. "We all want to know who sent such lovely flowers."

Louise hesitated, then slipped a slender card from its envelope and read: "Many thanks, Dan Lefcowitz."

"Who is this Dan Lefcowitz? Where did you meet him?" demanded Ricki, who as her best friend knew there had been no man in Louise's life since Mike.

"Stop imagining things. Just a grateful parent."

As she walked down the crowded hallways enjoying the admiring glances of teachers and students, the flowers felt like a validation of her ability to make things right. In her office, she perched the flowers on the metal filing cabinet where no careless student could knock them over. She wondered what sort of man sent such an opulent display to a school employee, someone he scarcely knew. Nevertheless, the generosity of his spirit hovered over the office, lifted her headache, and made her transcript work less onerous. She thought of the living being behind each transcript request, the hopes and dreams of each student, the nervousness as the student crossed the graduation stage in June, unfettered from school rules and parental control, pretending to know what to do next. With each thud of the school seal, she stamped her best wishes on the transcript.

During lunch, the line of students moved slowly through her office, each crisis deserving its telling before Louise could document the required action and administer a dose of compassion. But when the bell rang for fifth period, Louise realized she had not seen one important face, the face that should have been at the front of the line, the face behind the bouquet, the face of star student Abe Lefcowitz.

———————

At 2 p.m., near the end of the school day, Mr. Lefcowitz called to ask what Abe had decided to do and how he could help.

"No sign of him," Louise said. "Not even a note on my front door when I went to the Main Office to pick up a lovely bouquet, which by the way is deeply appreciated, Mr. Lefcowitz. I was a bit surprised. Both by the beautiful flowers you sent and by Abe's no-show."

"And you didn't call him down?" Mr. Lefcowitz demanded.

"I was giving him a chance to come on his own."

"I'm going to text him immediately to see what happened."

"If you don't mind a suggestion, Mr. Lefcowitz, maybe a face-to-face chat would be better." The pause on the other end of the line made her think that she had overstepped her bounds. "But you're the father. You know your son far better than I do."

Dan cleared his throat, then softly added, "I thought I did, Mrs. Krauss."

She wanted to reach across the phone line and pat his hand or nod with understanding. She yearned to tell him, "They're all inscrutable—all the kids. Especially when they're in high school. Like my daughter." But she had said more than enough.

Even after the conversation ended, Dan and his sadness lingered. She imagined him at a large wooden desk in a richly paneled office, his face drooping atop his stiff collar and his Windsor-knot tie. He had everything. And yet…who ever really knew what was going on in a child's mind? She could see Dan in a meeting with his assistant, likely the person who had actually ordered the bouquet, as he doodled the names of Tufts, Penn, and Colgate on his legal pad. Later he would drive home thinking of Abe and how to start the conversation at dinner, served in the dining room by Mrs. Lefcowitz—though Louise couldn't recall Dan mentioning Abe's mother. Out of curiosity, Louise pulled up Abe's student records. No siblings. No emergency number except Dan's. There would be just two at the table—Dan and Abe—and likely some carryout food on paper plates. No one else to help monitor and steer the conversation. She checked Abe's schedule, noted that he was in computer programming class, and jotted down the room number. It was time to play backup.

LOUISE DIDN'T REMEMBER WHAT ABE LOOKED LIKE—IT
had been months since he had submitted his application
packets—but she was expecting a tall boy, like his father,
dressed in preppy clothes that signaled where he had come
from and where he was headed. The short, slim boy with an
explosion of freckles over a pale face caught her off guard,
as did his athletic pants and rumpled t-shirt.

"You sent for me?" he said with coiled stillness.

"Abe Lefcowitz?"

"That's who they say I am."

"Hi, Abe. Come on in. Have a seat. I'm Mrs. Krauss."

"So your name plate tells me." He sat in the same chair
Dan had sat in, but unlike his father whose body had folded
over in grief, Abe pitched his body forward and claimed
her desk with his elbows. He stared at Louise, as she in turn
studied the boy and his whole affect before deciding how
to say what needed to be said.

"Do you know why I've called you down?"

"I can guess."

"Well, guess."

Abe pointed at the bouquet. "Mr. Daniel Lefcowitz,"
he said. "He loves to send flowers to people he thinks can
help me."

"Did he tell you about our conversation yesterday?"

"At least ten times."

"And how are you feeling about that?"

"What's done is done. The colleges have made up their
minds. I'm not the right fit for them. I'm done playing the
college game. At least for now." He slipped out his vibrating
cell phone, which should have been turned off per school

rules, and appeared to read a text. "Ah, it's him. *Go see Mrs. Krauss. Now.*" Abe returned the phone to his pocket and began tapping the desk with his thumbs as if he were texting, maybe what he wanted to say to his father, maybe what he was thinking.

"I want to help you, Abe, but only if you want my help."

"I don't need help, Mrs. Krauss. I'm managing just fine." His thumb movement continued rhythmically on the edge of Louise's desk.

"Your father cares very much about you."

"True."

"You've worked very hard to get to this moment, and you've had spectacular success along the way."

"Spectacular is a bit overstated, don't you think?"

"Then let's call it *significant success.*"

"Call it what you like. The college season's over. The results are in. Look, Mrs. Krauss, the buses will be coming soon. If you've got a point to make, maybe now's the time to make it."

His arrogance and nonstop tapping suggested swirling currents beneath the studied indifference of his clothes. Louise could tell he was a master at controlling the situation not unlike his father, though they appeared to be steering in different directions. He was rushing the pace of the conversation, hoping to throw her off balance, pushing for a quick escape from an uncomfortable reality.

"Have a chocolate." She tossed a Hershey's kiss in his direction, then watched him reflexively remove the foil and pop the candy into his mouth. She tossed another, then smiled.

The thumb tapping stopped as his body partly uncoiled into the chair. Now is the time to speak, she thought.

"You still have choices to make, Abe, and good colleges that will find a place for you, and a good future around the corner. I'll be glad to work with you to help make that happen this year, but I need your permission."

"Hey, Mrs. Krauss, I can see you're a nice lady, a caring lady, but I fixed it this way."

"You fixed what?"

"The admissions. I fixed it so I wouldn't be accepted. I wrote a college essay that I knew would doom me."

She said nothing, letting the sound of his confession echo in the office and rebound off the metal file cabinet with the floral offering.

"You wouldn't understand," he said.

"Try me."

"He wanted me to go so badly, but his business is struggling. I saw the unpaid bills on his nightstand—for the nursing home where my mom is, for the mortgage, for the electricity, for the car, for the credit card bills filled with charges for clothing and food and...flowers. If I got into one of those schools, he'd do whatever he had to do to send me—lose the house, his business. Now's not the time for me to go to college, but I knew he wouldn't listen. So I sabotaged the applications. I made the decision irrevocable. And now you're trying to undo it."

Ah, Louise thought, Abe was just a child, who despite his brilliance and his efforts at control, had self-destructed in order to be his father's savior. Now his rash actions had made the task of righting his life so much harder. What ugly things had he written in the essays to seal his fate? There would be so many more hoops to jump through to reopen the doors to college—not just for now, but for next year or the year after that, explanations he would have to address in future essays, additional letters from counselors, teachers, herself, Dan. Dan who was waiting to hear Abe's decision, eager to get started, still married to a dream that Abe had deliberately shredded.

"You owe it to your father to tell him."

"It's better for him to think crazy things just happened during the admissions process. He would be upset that I worried about his money. I can just tell him I need some time off to work, to clear my head about the rejections before trying again."

Louise wondered if Dan had truly been oblivious to Abe's ambivalence about the applications to these elite colleges or if he had ignored the signs, afraid to press for answers in case his questions pushed his son away or revealed something he didn't want to know about his son's life. Like she hadn't pressed Sammi about the razor when it slid from her backpack with her failing history test.

"Gotta go," Abe announced as the bell rang. "And don't forget to keep quiet about this. I'll tell the story in my own way." Before Louise could prod him to reconsider, he was racing down the hall with the frenetic throngs. She knew the phone would soon ring, and it would be Dan, the urgency in his voice intensified by his son's inaction. He would demand to know what Abe had said, what Louise and Abe had concluded, what would happen today and tomorrow and the day after that, how certain she was that the situation could be fixed, confirmation that life would go on as planned. She could encourage them to talk—set up an appointment with the counselor or an outside professional, but she couldn't tell Abe's story. Abe was right—it was his story to tell. What would Dan do in the face of his son's refusal to follow path B? And Abe, who thought he was being so clever by gaming the system, how would he feel when he realized he had actually made his father's life worse?

But Louise couldn't forget the image of the coiled boy who had entered her office and drummed incessantly on her desk. Something in that image suggested that the lie Abe had prepared for Dan's consumption was actually the truth, that Abe's self-sabotage had not been to protect Dan, that Abe had been tightly wound for so long that he was unraveling and needed time to breathe. So he had lied to himself and to Louise about his motivation for self-sabotage. What a complicated mess, Louise thought.

Her head began to throb again, a vise squeezing her forehead until the pain radiated to the back of her head, pinching the base of her neck. She no longer saw Abe. Instead, she saw Sammi pulling her history test from her backpack and her eyes filling with fear as a sliver of metal fell to the floor. Sammi retrieving the razor and announcing, "For an art project." Sammi tucking it into the backpack and pulling down the left sleeve of her hoodie. Sammi crying, "I failed my history exam. It will destroy my GPA forever." Louise wrapping her arms around Sammi, telling her no one's future was destroyed by one test. Sammi retreating to her bedroom with her backpack. Louise knocking on the door before bedtime and asking Sammi if everything was okay. Sammi insisting, "It's fine, Mom." Louise tossing and turning in bed, then rising for work, assuming that Sammi would be just fine, that the bumps of the past few months were just bumps, that she would surely know if Sammi were floundering.

She hadn't asked about the razor or confiscated it. She hadn't insisted that Sammi roll up her sleeves.

The phone rang. It was Mr. Lefcowitz, pleading in desperation, "I don't understand what's happening. What am I to do?"—a question she could no longer answer with assurance. She flipped the school phone to speaker and took out her cell phone. *Coming home early*, she texted Sammi. *Let's talk.*

Mr. Lefcowitz's voice filled the room, "Mrs. Krauss, are you there?" But she was somewhere else.

She imagined herself dashing into her house, calling, "Sammi, I'm home," hurrying upstairs to the purple room with the lavender duvet and the picture of Katy Perry. She was hugging Sammi, and then casually pushing up the sleeves of her daughter's hoodie and massaging her wrists, probing for scars—puffy or thin, solo or clustered, old or fresh. All the while praying and waiting for when Sammi wasn't looking and she could drop her eyes to Sammi's wrists and see what had to be the truth. The dewy skin of her daughter, unblemished but for a dark freckle on the inside of her left wrist.

Thieves

Bella was working the front register at CVS the first time she saw the blur of a short figure in an oversized Washington Caps hoodie vanishing with a pack of Skittles. One and done, she told herself. No need to alert the manager. But the second time, as she was shelving skin creams, she managed to glimpse the same figure and the delight in the boy's smile as he escaped with his Skittles. On both occasions, he was alone—no older brother or sister nearby, no mother or father at the prescription counter picking up antibiotics. He looked about seven, an age when a kid shouldn't be visiting stores on his own. And the fact that the snatching had happened twice with the boy all alone suggested that he was used to being unattended and that he would likely try again.

Still, Bella hesitated to tell the manager, or even to alert her good friend, Enrique, the senior cashier. They would be forced by store policy to contact the boy's parents and who knew what they were like—maybe they beat their kids with belts. Were two packs of Skittles really worth a beating? After all, she reasoned, how much profit was CVS losing on a $1.49 package of candy?

But Bella knew that if someone else caught the boy the next time—like the scowling cashier who reminded Bella of her mother—the boy would be reported. She remembered when her mother had called her a thief for borrowing cash from Ericka's wallet a couple times to help out her ex-boyfriend Stone. As if borrowing money without permission from your own mother and intending to pay it back eventually was criminal. As if taking a pack of Skittles made a seven-year-old a thief.

On the other hand, Bella reasoned, the boy shouldn't go unchecked in his actions. First candy, next a package of batteries, then a tablet from the electronics shop next door. By ignoring his impulsive candy grabs, she could be contributing to a life of crime, or at least a stay in the juvenile detention system. Both candy incidents had happened midday—about noon—probably on a half-day of school, as he took a detour home from nearby Shadyside Elementary. That night she pulled up the public school calendar online, identified the next half-day, and circled the date on her own calendar.

BELLA RECOGNIZED THE FADED, MISSHAPEN RED HOODIE before the face. It was swallowing the boy, making him smaller and more fragile than his cunning suggested as he hung around the candy display, watching and waiting for a line to form at her register.

"Hey," she called out. "Kid, is this yours?" She pulled a package of Skittles from her pocket and waved it in his direction. He turned away and started to run toward the door, but she moved more quickly and blocked his exit, her hand outstretched with the candy offering. He reached for it, but she yanked it back.

"I'll pay for the Skittles if you promise not to snatch anymore candy from the store."

"What if you're not here? If somebody else is up front?"

"Then you wait until I'm here another time. I'm trusting you not to take anything else. Besides, if someone else catches you, they'll call your mother."

"Don't live with her anymore."

"Well, they'll call whoever you are living with. And all bets are off then."

"Huh?"

"They'll call the police if you keep doing it."

"I'm very fast. They'll never catch me."

"Then you don't know Enrique. He used to run track in high school. Kid, this is an easy decision. Don't make it hard. Skittles when I'm here, nothing when I'm not. And no punishment."

He nodded and reached for the candy, ripping open the package and stuffing pieces in his mouth before they could be reclaimed. "Whas your name?" he asked with the sweetness filling his mouth.

"Bella. What's yours?"

"Jamal." His dark fringed eyes sparkled as he smiled, pastel saliva dribbling from the corner of his mouth. "Where's Enrique? The man who's so fast?"

Bella pointed to a short, thin guy at the pharmacy register at the back of the store.

"Doesn't look like a runner."

"He still runs on weekends. You should see his calves."

But before they could finish their conversation about honesty and stealing, Enrique's voice boomed over the intercom, "Bella to the front register please." And just like that, Jamal was gone.

"Do you want me to lose my job, or do you want me to fire you?" Enrique demanded as they rode home shoulder to shoulder in his 2008 Corolla, which he'd bought from his aunt so he'd have reliable transportation. Bella could tell something had been boiling in him all day, his required CVS smile having been replaced by a half-frown. They were friends, good friends, roommates—on the same wave length most of the time, but now the harshness in his voice reminded her of her mother.

"You can't be wandering away from the register. Leaving it unattended invites anyone to come up and open the drawer. Thieves watch for moments like that. And what were you doing anyway giving that kid candy? It's not a Halloween promotion day. The last thing we need is little kids hanging around the store begging for free candy. By the way, you owe CVS $1.49. The manager gets angry when the candy inventory doesn't match the sales receipts."

Bella said nothing. She had no place else to live at the low rent Enrique and his boyfriend were charging her, especially while she was saving for summer classes.

"Promise me you won't step away again like that. You're my best friend, Bella. But it's my job to enforce CVS rules." His voice had become softer, almost pleading.

"I promise," she said. "By the way, I don't steal. I put the money in the register and rang up the sale." She silently reminded herself to put the money in the drawer the next morning.

That night as the heater hissed and rattled, Bella fidgeted on the wafer-thin futon, feeling each fragile slat as she thought about Jamal, who seemed as rootless as she.

Only he was seven with his permanent teeth just popping up, and she was almost twenty—earning her own money, taking college classes, strong enough to get herself out of a bad relationship with Stone, who she sometimes missed at night when she heard Enrique and Owen in the bedroom. Why was a kid wandering on his own like that? Did anyone care where he was or what was happening to him? If Skittles made him happy, didn't life owe it to him?

When Enrique was in a better mood, she'd explain, and he would understand. But at breakfast Enrique let slip that CVS would be downsizing soon, that the receipts didn't justify the salary expenditures, that they couldn't reduce the professional pharmacy staff, that the manager was under pressure himself, that Enrique was doing his best to protect both their jobs.

She squeezed his hand. "Don't worry about me," she said.

It was a Saturday morning, not when she expected to see him. At first Bella didn't even notice him amidst the gaggle of noisy kids being prodded past the toy section toward the pharmacy counter by a round woman with wiry hair. But when he called out, "Hi, Bella!" her heart pumped so fast that she forgot to scan her customer's chips.

"Hi, Bella," he shouted a second time, then dissolved into a spasm of coughing as the woman jerked his hoodie. "No playing around, Jamal," she ordered. "You're the one who needs the medicine." He turned and waved enthusiastically as the woman dragged him along with the rest of her crew. Bella offered a half-wave, then turned to her customer, an older man who stopped by regularly for corn chips and pain patches.

"See you soon, Bella," the boy yelled from the back of the store.

Bella handed the man his bag, making sure not to crush the chips. She remembered her deal with Jamal—free Skittles if she was there, no snatching if she wasn't. Relieved that Enrique had a big crowd at the pharmacy counter and that no other customers were in her line, she reached over the counter, plucked a pack of Skittles, and surreptitiously tossed it across the freshly waxed floor like a hockey puck until it rested just shy of the exit. Jamal, who had been staring at her, dashed toward the skidding candy, slid in like a goalie to retrieve the package, and triumphantly jammed colored candies into his mouth.

"Jamal! Where'd you get that candy, boy? Are you stealing again? And now you've gone and tore it open. Do you think I've got extra money to waste on candy? You walk over to that girl and give her back what's left of that stuff. Then you promise to pay her for what's missing when you earn it. You heard me, Jamal. Get your tail over there." The woman was now standing over the boy and shaking her finger at him, as if she were shaking his little body.

The gaggle of kids had followed her and were laughing. "Jamal's done it again!"

"She gave me the candy." Jamal was pointing at Bella. "She promised me."

"Stop your lying. Give her back that candy if you know what's good for you."

By then Enrique was walking toward the commotion, close enough to hear every word, approaching the woman but glaring at Bella, who shrugged her shoulders and whispered the word, "Sorry."

"I'm not lying. She tossed it on the floor so I could get it." Bella wanted to tell the truth, but how do you explain to a furious woman that you were giving her boy free candy without having her think you're a pedophile? What was left of the candy pieces tumbled to the ground, rolled under the display case for Mother's Day candy and artificial flowers, and buried themselves in dust balls. The other kids dove to the floor and wedged their hands beneath the case, shouting their color preferences as grit covered their hands. As Enrique's focus shifted toward the squirming craziness on the floor, Jamal scowled at Bella, then zipped out the front door.

"Damn that boy!" shouted the round woman.

Enrique raced out the door, in track team mode, and Bella knew what would come next: Enrique would catch Jamal in seconds and return him to the woman, who would deliver another loud lecture, and Bella would be out of a job and off the futon. But before she could feel victimized by fate and her own stupidity, a car squealed in the front lot and horns blared. Shit! she thought. Who had she killed—the boy or Enrique? And for what? Candy that was no longer edible.

SHE HAD BECOME AN ACCOMPLICE IN JAMAL'S CANDY hustle. Maybe her mother was right that she was a thief at heart. But when she hugged Jamal's warm body in relief that he was safe, her heart swelled as if he were her little brother. The round woman pulled Jamal away, and he jutted his defiant chin in rebuke while Bella explained her actions to his disbelieving caregiver. Bella longed to enfold him again in her arms and give him the love he deserved, the kind of love she'd imagined as a child. His cough and leaky nose made him even more vulnerable, more in need of caring, not punishment.

Thank goodness, no one had been killed, not even injured. Enrique and the boy were sweaty and angry, but nothing that wouldn't right itself soon. The squealing car and blaring horns had been warnings to the wild boy racing between cars in the parking lot and to Enrique sprinting after him. And now, she realized, warnings to herself as well for making her own rules. Enrique, who had been promoted to head cashier for good reason, calmed the woman long enough to offer profuse apologies on behalf of the store, along with discount coupons and candy for each of the kids, even Skittles for Jamal. Then Enrique dashed to the pharmacy to hand-carry the medicine to the seething woman just as she loaded the children into her van, giving Jamal—the last to board—an extra shove and two butt-swats.

During the handover of the free medicine, another courtesy of the pharmacy, Bella managed to write her cell number on a piece of paper and slip it into Jamal's hand. "If you need help," she whispered, "call me." It was the least she could do. She imagined what would happen after the woman and the kids were behind closed doors. The woman's anger at Jamal had been palpable throughout the entire scene—from the moment they'd entered the store, to the moment they'd finally buckled up in the van. Bella would never forgive herself if Jamal got smacked around because of her careless generosity, especially with him so congested, maybe even feverish. She waved at him as the van backed out of its space, and she thought she saw him stick out his tongue as they pulled away.

Enrique eyeballed Bella as if he had something important to say, then shook his head. "Sweep up those Skittles," he said. "Then go home."

"Sorry," she said again, something she was saying much too frequently. She watched as he took over the front register and used just the right words to apologize to the people waiting for service, forcing a smile but looking defeated, as if her failures had become his as well.

Back at Enrique's apartment, she jammed her CVS jacket into the trashcan and released her curls from her work-required scrunchie. As a parting gift to her friend, she washed and dried the breakfast dishes still in the sink, cleaned the bathroom shower so none of her hair clogged the drain, and smoothed the wrinkles her body had made on the futon cover. Then she packed her clothes in her duffle bag and rested her pillow from home next to the luggage, just as she had done a couple months ago when she moved from the room she had shared with Stone. She owed Enrique and Owen half a month's rent, and she would repay CVS from her paycheck for the medicine and candy. She also owed Enrique a face-to-face, a chance to give her hell—not just for her initial carelessness but for lying when she told him not to worry.

Now she realized she owed her mother, too. She'd never paid back the money she'd taken to help out Stone. It hadn't seemed like much each time she'd slipped a twenty from her mother's wallet, and her mother's oversized rage had convinced Bella that repayment wasn't deserved. Was it too late to slide an envelope with the money into her mother's mailbox?

"I was getting worried," she told Enrique when he stepped through the door at 7 p.m. She'd been waiting for hours, so long that she'd made and unmade temporary sleeping plans three times.

"I've been meeting with the manager and other stuff." Enrique collapsed on the leather chair and propped his feet on her duffle bag, saying nothing about her carefully organized belongings.

"And?" she asked.

"The boss is letting you go, Bella. I tried, but with the downsizing...."

"You didn't need to try. It was all my fault—the whole mess. Is your job safe?"

"For now. He liked how I handled the mother and the police officer."

"The police? You called the police on Jamal?"

"Hell no. The police came by about you. What were you thinking when you gave the kid your phone number? The woman was convinced you were some kind of pervert out to harm the boy. She called Social Services, who called the police. It took me and the manager an hour to explain what really happened and what a nice girl you are and how generally reliable.... "

"The police?" she said as a cold chill swept over her.

"What did you expect? An officer's outside the apartment in his squad car, doing a background check on you."

"Oh, shit, shit, shit." She buried her face in her pillow, hoping to block out the reality she'd created. Everything was unraveling, and for this latest catastrophe, she couldn't blame her mother or Stone. Every step she took forward in life threw her off balance and jerked other people off balance with her. Enrique had hired her, given her rides to school, helped edit her English papers, given her a safe place to live, trusted her. "I'll be out of here tonight," she told Enrique as she lifted her face. "You don't deserve this."

Then Enrique was holding her tight in his sturdy arms, like she'd held Jamal, squeezing her as if his hug would quiet everything swirling around inside her. "You may have fucked up," he told her, "but you're not going anywhere."

She rested her head against him and breathed in his latte breath and the spicy aftershave that Owen liked so much and the detergent fragrance of his work jacket that she'd laundered yesterday. No one had forgiven her before or embraced her with all her flaws or become an anchor when logic said to throw her out. Enrique wanted her to stay. She belonged here.

Fairy Tales and Ghost Stories

Yesterday in her mailbox Ericka found six crisp twenty dollar bills in an envelope labeled *Mother* in careful cursive, the presentation elevating the cash to a ceremonial offering, as if it weren't enough just to repay the money. The word *Mother*, of course, was superfluous. The exact amount in the exact denominations that Bella had secretly removed from Ericka's wallet over the course of six weeks had been enough to identify the sender. Bella, whom she had loved more than anyone in the world after Ev had betrayed Ericka. Bella, who had squandered Ericka's love through her theft for Stone, a worthless bum.

What did Bella look like? Ericka wondered. Had she kept her hair curly or straightened it like the flat-ironed hair of the young women on t.v.? Those frivolous, freedom-loving curls that resisted Ericka's best efforts at sprays and clips when Bella was little—Bella had become like the curls themselves, resistant to control. Was she still with Stone? Had she made anything of herself, or was she bumping through life? Why had she finally repaid the money? The cascading questions had prevented Ericka from calling Bella herself, afraid that she would ask them all at once and provoke Bella to hang up. Soon they would be face-to-face, and she hoped she could control her tongue and keep open the possibility of reconciliation.

"You'll know what to say," her friend Louise told Ericka. It was Louise who had called Bella, Louise who had set up the meeting, Louise who knew how to make things right.

Now Ericka was cleaning and straightening. Though Bella herself wouldn't mind a few out of order items, if the room were disheveled, she'd get the message that Ericka didn't care. She fluffed each cushion with a firm whack, angled the knickknacks on the coffee table to create a focus, dusted the lampshades to remove invisible dust. Then she stopped in front of the breakfront, her hand hovering over the linen drawer where a second envelope rested, and surveyed the room. The sweetness of freshly baked crumb cake mingled with the scent of brewing coffee.

Who would believe a story about an estranged daughter suddenly reaching out to her mother? Ericka wondered. She had cast Bella out in anger two years ago, derived—Ericka now understood—from Ericka's displaced anger at others. Anger at Ev for his infidelity and then dying before he could atone. Anger, too, at Mutter for turning away when Ericka was left widowed with a small child. So much pain in one life. So much possibility in one meeting.

The old Ericka would have snarled, "I don't believe the story for one minute. It's a fairy tale." The new Ericka, who had discovered possibilities in her mailbox, would respond, "Life can bring unspeakable tragedies, but it can also bring astounding miracles."

The doorbell was ringing. Her throat tightened, her breath became shallow. There she was, standing on the other side of the door. Bella.

THE ALMOST-SAMENESS OVERWHELMED HER. THE FLORAL sofa with the fluffed cushions where Bella dared not put her feet. The crystal bowl from Berlin, moved now from the coffee table to the breakfront in the dining room. Mother's pale blue dress that she wore at Bella's high school graduation and her gray hair sprayed into submission, with a strange dustball clinging to the top. Bella's stomach churned like it had when she'd missed curfew and found Mother waiting, hands on hips, in the living room. Repaying the money should wipe out what she owed Mother. What about what Mother owed her?

"Bella…how good to see you…won't you…won't you come in." The tightness of Mother's voice, the hesitant formality of her words, felt unnatural, as if Bella were a visitor in her school office, not her daughter.

"I can't stay long," Bella announced. "I've got a friend waiting for me outside in the car."

"But you'll stay long enough to talk. And cake. Yes, long enough for some of my crumb cake."

"Not too long. He's got to be somewhere in twenty minutes."

"So stingy with time that conniver Stone is…." Mother stopped, then started again, her voice an octave higher, the words sing-song like a rehearsed message. "That I shouldn't have said. I apologize. Whoever is in the car, wherever he needs to be, that is your business. We each have our own business."

Bella didn't correct Mother's misconception or mention that she hadn't seen Stone for months. She just stared at the ridiculous dustball stuck in the middle of Ericka's hair like a cartoon bird dropping, until a giggle slipped out with a hiss.

"So it is funny to you that I apologize? Two years it's taken for me to begin to understand you and me."

"And what do you understand?" demanded Bella. "That I've disappointed you at every turn?"

"No more of this. Come, have cake." Mother ushered her into the kitchen where two blue and white china plates and cloth napkins rested on embroidered place mats. Bella sat directly across from Mother, as it had been forever, at a table haunted by a missing father. For years, she had no full name to attach to him—just Papa, which she stopped saying aloud to Mother whose face banned the word.

Ericka cut an extra-large piece of cake and leaned slightly to place it on Bella's plate, causing the dustball to float from her hair onto the crumb cake. Bella pointed. "That's what was making me giggle. This dustball on your hair, so unlike you." Mother laughed, first forcing the laughter, then giving in to the absurdity of the situation.

"Not so bad to laugh once in a while," Mother said.

She turned to the sink, puttering with something Bella couldn't see, her back bent over, then pivoted with a hot pink cupcake and a single lit candle. "A delicious cupcake bought just for you. Your twentieth birthday, last week, I didn't forget. Happy birthday to you, happy birthday to you. Happy birthday, dear Bella. Happy birthday to you."

Bella felt like gagging as she blew out the candle. The hint of acrid burning lingered, like every September 11 when Bella hid behind the sofa and watched Ericka scorch a letter over the sink. She knew better than to ask about the strange ritual. But one year, growing bold, Bella checked the mailbox daily for weeks before September 11, searching for a letter that might drive her mother to destroy it and then destroy even its ashes. Finally, on a sultry August day when her mother was tied up late at the school office, Bella found an official letter from the Pentagon addressed to Mrs. Ericka Rogers and family. She held the letter up to the light and strained to see what words terrified her mother, until frustrated by its opaqueness, she returned the envelope to the mailbox.

Bella stared at the extinguished candle. "Thanks for remembering," she said.

"How could I forget? In the hospital, I held your bundled body, nervous but full of joy."

"And Papa? He was there?"

Mother turned away again and poured steaming coffee into two china cups.

"And Papa?" Bella repeated with emphasis.

"Enough. Not now."

Mother had always bought a supermarket cupcake with synthetic icing for an all-American celebration of Bella's birthday. Each year Bella had pretended to enjoy the cloying sweetness until finally, in high school the cupcake came to symbolize Mother's deflection of the truth, and Bella left it half-eaten on the plate. That was after she had learned in history class about the 9/11 attack on the Pentagon and connected the attack to the arrival of the letter. On a school computer, she discovered a Pentagon website honoring the victims, and there on its list was the name that had to be his—Randall Everett Rogers, LT—her Papa, whose arms had lifted her high above his head until he evaporated. Now the cupcake sickened her.

"I don't care for the icing. It's too artificial for my taste." Bella pumped the last sentence with extra force and watched Mother flinch at the zinger. She pushed her thumb into the cupcake, icing splattering on the place mat, then felt juvenile for having mutilated the innocent cupcake.

"Bella, if the icing doesn't suit you, just let it alone." Mother's firm voice evoked years of skirmishes.

"I can't. It reminds me of an empty table." Mother's eyes darkened and her cheeks collapsed, erasing Bella's momentary triumph and reminding Bella of her own sadness. Why hadn't she noticed Mother's sadness when she lived here? Why hadn't Mother noticed hers? As silence consumed the room, Bella forced herself to stay, knowing the answer she had always wanted would elude her if she left. She studied Ericka frantically brushing crumbs into a napkin, that single image capturing the essence of Mother—cleaning, puttering, hiding life's messes.

"You're not a bad girl," Mother said as she rubbed icing from a place mat. "You paid back the money, a big surprise to me, a good thing to do." Mother looked up, her eyes forming a question—can you forgive me?—a question Bella couldn't answer.

"Shit, what a left-handed compliment."

"But you came today, even though it was hard. You didn't know what I'd say or do. Still, you walked through that door to face me. What strength you have, Bella."

"This doesn't sound like you, this gushy stuff about me. Not even calling me out for cussing. Remember, I'm the girl who stole from your wallet and pretended to myself that I borrowed it and gave your money to Stone and lied to myself that he would shape up. We both know you were right. I was a thief at heart. And Stone was a worthless user."

"I was a thief, too. I stole from you."

"No kidding!" Bella cackled. "That's what Stone told me when we were together."

"That's not Stone waiting outside?"

"Hell no. Stone's out of my life."

"He's gone? He's left you?"

"No, I left him."

"Well, Bella, I underestimated you for certain." Mother smiled, then bit her lower lip to conceal her delight. She walked to the dining room and with a flourish, opened the linen drawer of the breakfront that contained something new on top of the tablecloths and cloth napkins that had traveled with her years ago from Germany. "There's a package you should see," she announced. Slowly, gently, she removed a large brown envelope labeled "Ericka and Bella." "For you, Bella," Mother said, her voice wavering. "An envelope more delinquent than the envelope you put in my mailbox."

Bella shivered as she accepted the envelope. What was inside? The handwriting was unfamiliar, the fading envelope wrinkled, its corners bent.

"Open it. You'll find something I've owed you for years."

Bella unfastened the foreign clasp, reached in, and pulled out a picture of a tall curly-haired man in a military uniform, his arm draped around a younger Ericka in a floral dress holding a bouquet of wild flowers. "Papa? I thought you threw away all the pictures of Papa."

"Our wedding day. Look. There's more."

Bella removed a second picture of the same curly-haired man, this time in a gray shirt and jeans sitting at a kitchen table with Ericka in a sundress, next to a highchair with a round-faced little girl—about one—her stray curls and hands coated with icing from a cupcake. "My first birthday. Papa, you, me."

"More, Bella. Look again."

She pulled out a letter, yellowed by age, but folded neatly, written to a woman named Gertrud by Papa, a man she had mostly forgotten, except for the firmness of his hands and the laughter in his voice. Words about her birth, how beautiful she was, how much he loved her and her mother, how he hoped to bring Bella to Germany to meet her grandmother Gertrud and see the places where he had fallen in love with her mother. Then more pictures tumbled out—Bella walking toward Papa's outstretched hands, Mother leaning against Papa's chest, a studio portrait of the three of them, Bella blowing a kiss at a laughing Papa—dozens of pictures of two years of her life. Her heart battered her lungs. For a full minute she couldn't think, couldn't breathe, until Mother stroked her back, and Bella exhaled.

"But you said there was nothing, no pictures anymore of him. All these years, you lied. You kept him from me when he was here all along."

"No lies, Bella. I had nothing. The pictures of him I threw away, cut him out of pictures with you, removed him from our lives. Too much pain because he cheated and told me days before the plane hit the Pentagon and killed him. But even when I made his pictures go away, the pain stayed. These pictures—all of them—are from Mutter, your grandmother, who hurt me, too. She passed away, and the envelope came only last month. All this she left for me, and for you."

"One more month of secrecy, compounding eighteen years of silence."

"I was overwhelmed by fresh pain about him, you, Mutter. Then the second envelope came—the one from you—a sign that I must tell you what I should have years ago. About Ev, your father. That I loved him. That he loved us both."

Randall Everett Rogers. Ev. Papa.

ERICKA STARED OUT THE LIVING ROOM WINDOW AT HER
daughter clutching the brown envelope as she walked to
the red Corolla where her friend waited to drive her home.
Their meeting hadn't gone as Ericka hoped. Things rarely
did. No warm embraces, no words of reconciliation. Still,
when she'd placed her hand on Bella's back, her daughter
hadn't flinched, and the lump in Ericka's chest that had
grown larger every year, had partially dissolved. She'd even
noticed a few tears in Bella's eyes, and Ericka herself had
felt on the verge once or twice.

As the car door popped open, Ericka saw shadows flit-
ting on the roof of the Corolla—or were they people? A big-
boned man with a familiar face was throwing his arms up as
if tossing a child in the air. Ev—the philanderer who loved
her. A woman with gray hair in a stingy bun clapped with
glee. Mutter. How could a mother seemingly incapable of
caring, in fact care? How could a man who loved her deeply
betray her? How could a daughter who stole from her fill
her heart with both anger and love? How could she shut
the door on people who wounded her, then open her heart
again? People were complicated creatures, that's for certain.

From the living room window, Ericka watched Bella
wave at the young man in the car, then turn to look back at
the house. Was she saying farewell or reclaiming memories?
Ericka thought she heard Bella call out, "I'll be back." Or
was that only wishful thinking, another fairy tale?

Then Bella slid into the front seat of the Corolla, and the
young man in the front seat turned on the engine and drove
away with Ev and Mutter clinging to the roof and laughing.

ACKNOWLEDGMENTS

My writing has its roots in my childhood with family members who nurtured my imagination and my love for words. Though they are now deceased, they live on in my heart and in my stories.

- My father, the man with the golden voice, who invested each word he spoke with intense meaning.

- My mother, who gave me space and time to explore my inner world, even when our house was overrun with the tumult of four children.

- My grandmother, who made me recite poems and find the beauty in words and who in later years wrote her own poems and memoirs in language far more sophisticated than her eighth-grade education.

- My aunt, who taught me to read and opened my mind to the world of books.

- My cousins Harriet and Mildred, who played paperdolls with me and spurred me to create my own stories.

Carol Solomon

In later years, when I retired from education and editing and immersed myself fulltime in creative writing, other writers encouraged my efforts.

- My son, an editorial director and award-winning writer, who generously calls me "the best writer in the family."

- My daughter, a technical writer and editor whose indomitable spirit inspires my work.

- My teachers Faye Moskowitz and Michelle Brafman, who convinced me that my words deserved more readers.

- Nora Gold, founder and editor of Jewish Fiction.Net, who published my first story and validated my work.

- Nechie King and Beth Greenfeld, whose honest critiques elevated these stories.

A very special thanks to the Arts and Humanities Council of Montgomery County, Maryland, which funded the publication of this collection and my outreach to senior groups. Their generosity and encouragement promote the creations of local authors, artists, and scholars. I am indeed fortunate to live in a community with taxpayers who value the arts and humanities.

Finally and most importantly, I am grateful to my husband, whose enduring love and companionship for fifty years nourish my heart and my soul.